NEVADA VIPERS' NEST

Even fully prepared for danger, Fargo flinched violently when a deafening racket of gunfire opened up only inches above his head. He fired two shots dead center on the shadowy form inside the room. Screams erupted from the rooms behind him as a body flopped heavily onto the floor beside him.

Fargo knocked the gun a few feet away from the man's hand and tugged him over just in time to watch the would-be killer's pig eyes lose their vital focus and then glaze over like glass when he gave up the ghost. Evidently one of Fargo's bullets had struck a major artery. In the shocked silence that followed the sudden outburst of gunfire, he could hear the obscene liquid-slapping sound of blood splashing onto the floor.

"Nice try," Fargo muttered.

THE

TRAILSMAN

#386

NEVADA VIPERS' NEST

by

Jon Sharpe

SIGNET
Published by the Penguin Group
Penguin Group (USA) LLC, 375 Hudson Street,
New York, New York 10014

USA | Canada | UK | Ireland | Australia | New Zealand | India | South Africa | China
penguin.com
A Penguin Random House Company

First published by Signet, an imprint of New American Library,
a division of Penguin Group (USA) LLC

First Printing, December 2013

The first chapter of this book previously appeared in *Thunderhead Trail*, the three
hundred eighty-fifth volume in this series.

Ⓟ REGISTERED TRADEMARK—MARCA REGISTRADA
ISBN 978-0-451-46550-4   *5250 3678*   12/13

Printed in the United States of America
10 9 8 7 6 5 4 3 2 1

The Trailsman

Beginnings . . . they bend the tree and they mark the man. Skye Fargo was born when he was eighteen. Terror was his midwife, vengeance his first cry. Killing spawned Skye Fargo, ruthless, cold-blooded murder. Out of the acrid smoke of gunpowder still hanging in the air, he rose, cried out a promise never forgotten.

The Trailsman they began to call him all across the West: searcher, scout, hunter, the man who could see where others only looked, his skills for hire but not his soul, the man who lived each day to the fullest, yet trailed each tomorrow. Skye Fargo, the Trailsman, the seeker who could take the wildness of a land and the wanting of a woman and make them his own.

Carson Valley, Nevada Territory, 1861—where Skye Fargo must track down an elusive, mysterious woman or be branded a murderer of women and children.

1

Skye Fargo's stallion always showed a distinctive quiver in his nostrils when he whiffed death.

And they had begun that quivering now as Fargo started to ascend a low ridge overlooking the remote Carson Valley at the western edge of the newly formed Nevada Territory.

Fargo expelled a weary, fluming sigh as he reined in. "Steady on, old campaigner," he told his nervous Ovaro. "You know that trouble never leaves us alone for very long."

The buckskin-clad man some called the Trailsman sat tall in the saddle, his alert lake blue eyes watching his surroundings from a weather-bronzed, crop-bearded face. He was wide in the shoulders, slim in the hips, and a dusty white hat left half his face in shadow.

The deadly alkali flats of Nevada stretched out to infinity behind him; the majestic, ascending folds of the California Sierra rose before him. Fargo was currently employed by the army as an express messenger between Camp Floyd in the Utah Territory and Fort Churchill in Nevada.

Normally his route would not take him this far west into the silver-mining country. But the Paiutes, Bannocks and Shoshones in this region—no tribes to fool with—had recently made common cause to war on whiteskins. Fargo had been forced to flee in this direction to shake a war party determined to lift his dander.

And now this new trouble . . .

"Caught between a sawmill and a shootout," Fargo muttered. "Story of my life."

He clucked at his nervous stallion and gigged him up to a trot, sliding his brass-framed Henry rifle from its boot. The ridge he now ascended was strewn with boulders, and

Fargo's slitted eyes stayed in constant scanning motion, watching for dry-gulchers.

Near the top of the ridge he spotted buzzards wheeling in a cloudless sky of bottomless blue—merchants of death impatient to feast. But the fact that they were still circling told Fargo that someone, human or animal, was likely still alive below.

Just before he topped the long ridge, he detected motion in the corner of his left eye.

With the honed reflexes of a civet cat, Fargo threw the reins forward and rolled from the saddle, levering a round into the Henry's chamber even before he landed on the ground. He peered cautiously past the Ovaro's shoulder, eyes widening in surprised disbelief.

In this dreary and woman-scarce country, the woman he now clearly spotted fleeing between boulders stood out like a brass spittoon in a funeral parlor. Evidently Fargo had ridden too close and scared her out of hiding.

"Hey!" he called out. "No need to skedaddle, lady! Maybe I can help you."

She paused for a moment, turning in his direction. Fargo drank in the thick tresses of copper-colored hair, flawless mother-of-pearl skin, a pretty, fine-boned face. But her sprigged-muslin dress was obscenely splotched with blood.

"What happened?" Fargo called to her, stepping out into the open.

By way of reply, the woman brought her right hand into view and fired a short iron at Fargo. The bullet came nowhere near him, but the surprised Trailsman leaped back behind his stallion.

"Christ, lady, lower the hammer! I want to help you. Are you hurt?"

"No, and I'm not going to be!" she shouted back. "If you even try to get any closer to me, I'm going to use every bullet but one in this gun to try to kill you. And if I miss, I'll use the last bullet on myself! I swear to God I will!"

The sheer desperation in her voice told Fargo she had recently suffered some unspeakable horror. He believed she meant every word.

"All right, lady, it's your call. But listen to me. If you turn to your right you'll be headed due south. Carson City is only three miles from here in that direction. If you keep going east like you are now, you'll die in the desert."

She must have heard him because she did turn south, disappearing among a clutch of boulders.

Fargo turned the stirrup, took up the reins and stepped up and over. A minute later he topped the ridge and saw the whole bloody chronicle, laid out below like a tableau straight from hell.

"Shit-oh-dear," he muttered, fighting to control his sidestepping stallion, who wanted nothing to do with the scene below.

A sudden squall of anger tightened Fargo's lips and facial muscles. Despite everything he had seen during his many years yondering on the western frontier, there were some things he had never learned to stomach.

Especially the brutal murder of women and children.

A burned-out prairie schooner, still sending up curls of smoke, lay on its side, six dead Cleveland Bays tangled in the traces, all shot through their heads. A man, a woman and two small girls lay scattered about like ninepins, bodies riddled with bullet holes. The woman's calico dress had been pulled up and her chemise and pantaloons ripped away—clearly she had been raped before she was murdered.

Fargo also saw why the buzzards were still wheeling instead of swooping in for the feast. A man stood beside a blaze-faced sorrel, his face ashen as he surveyed the grisly scene.

"Rider coming in!" Fargo called out, bringing his Henry down to the level.

The man scarcely seemed to hear or notice the new arrival, still staring around him in a state of shock.

"Mister, you're either an innocent passerby or one damn fine actor," Fargo greeted him as he dismounted.

The man said nothing to this, his unblinking eyes like two glazed marbles. Fargo gave him a quick size-up. He was of medium height and build with a homely, careworn face and an unruly shock of dark hair. With his usual abundance of caution, Fargo kept the Henry leveled on him, but he strongly doubted that the stranger had played a hand in this slaughter.

Fargo glanced at the unusual firearm tucked behind the man's canvas belt.

"I see you play the harmonica," Fargo said, meaning the harmonica pistol the man carried. "Mind if I take a look at it?"

Fargo knew damn well that a small-caliber pistol didn't do the killing here. The dead man's heart had practically been ripped out of his body by a large-bore weapon. But the Trailsman hadn't survived so long by coming to quick conclusions.

"Snap out of your shit!" Fargo barked when the man failed to respond. "I said let me glom that harmonica."

Fargo's take-charge voice did rouse the man from his stupor. He handed the weapon over. It was an early attempt at a multishot pistol. A sliding bar held ten bullets with primer caps, the mechanism roughly resembling a harmonica. Each time the weapon was fired, the bar could be slid to the next round. The harmonica pistol had never caught on, though, because it was awkward and cumbersome.

"All right, mister," Fargo said, handing the weapon back, "give."

"Not much to give," he replied. "I just got here about ten minutes before you did. I didn't see or hear anything."

"What brings you to these parts?"

"You might say I had to take the geographic cure, and in a puffin' hurry. I was working as a trick-whip performer for Dr. Geary's traveling medicine show. We were up north in Virginia City on the Comstock. I got into a poker game and somehow a fifth ace turned up."

"Musta been a faulty deck," Fargo said sarcastically. "Where you headed?"

"Just drifting through to Old Sac," he replied, meaning Sacramento.

"What's your name?"

"Mitt McDougall, but I prefer to be called Sitch."

"Sitch . . . that's an unusual handle," Fargo remarked absently, beginning to study the ground around them for sign.

"It's bobtail for troublesome 'situations,' which I always find myself in—just like this one. Katy Christ, mister, did Indians do this?"

4

"Not unless they've taken to riding iron-shod horses and rolling cigarettes. There's several fresh butts here."

"And they call the red men savages. If it was road agents or whatever, why in Sam Hill did they have to slaughter all these folks just to rob them?"

"That don't cipher," Fargo agreed. "I've never heard of road agents deliberately killing women and children. Even the hardest of the hard twists shy away from that. Well, we best try to find out who these folks were before we bury them."

So far Fargo had avoided looking at the victims, but now he steeled himself for what must be done. He grounded his Henry, knelt beside the dead man and started searching through his pockets.

Suddenly, the Ovaro gave his trouble whicker.

Fargo started to reach for his rifle when a shot split the silence, a geyser of sand spurning up only inches from his feet.

"Both you murdering sons-a-bitches freeze!" shouted a gravelly voice that brooked no defiance. "Make one damn move and we'll shoot you to rag tatters!"

2

Fargo watched three men emerge from behind the huge granite boulders that rimmed Carson Valley, their horses walking slowly closer.

"What's those red sashes tied to their belts?" McDougall muttered. "Are they lawmen?"

"Jackleg lawmen," Fargo replied in a low voice. "They call themselves regulators—most are vigilante trash. Likely they rule the roost at the silver-mining camp near here, place called Rough and Ready."

"Shut your damn fish traps," ordered the man who had just spoken. "It's too late now for you murdering shit heels to get your story straight. We caught you red-handed."

The speaker was a muscular, big-framed man with long greasy hair tied into a knot. He wore a necklace made of grizzly claws. More ominously, he also wore a pair of ivory-handled Navy Colts, one aimed at Fargo. He swung down and approached closer on foot. Fargo noticed how his eyes seemed to trap a man like lance points.

"Listen up real good, buckskins. Real slow like, unbuckle that gun belt. And even slower, shuck that Arkansas toothpick from your boot and lay it next to the gun. Soon as you got that done, move away from the weapons. Before you try any fox play, you best take a good gander at the hardware aimed at you."

Fargo already had. One of the regulators siding the leader held an old Hawken rifle. Although now considered a relic of the mountain-man era, the formidable weapon was capable of dropping a buffalo at a thousand yards. Fargo had once seen a half-ounce ball fired from a Hawken remove half of a man's head.

The other regulator held a Sharps fifty in the crook of his left arm.

The leader's head swiveled toward Sitch McDougall. "And you with the hangdog face—toss down that harmonica gun or you'll be sucking wind."

Both men complied.

"Romer," the leader ordered the man with the Sharps fifty, "ground your long gun and search both these murdering bastards for hideout guns."

Fargo pegged the man called Romer as the sneakiest of the trio. He was ferret-faced with swift-as-minnow eyes, coarse-grained skin and broken teeth stained the color of licorice spit.

"They're both clean, Iron Mike," he said a minute later after patting both men down.

"Well, believe you me, assholes," Iron Mike told his prisoners, "both of you murderers will soon stretch hemp."

"I ain't never seen anything to equal it, Mike," said the third man, a skinny rake with green-rimmed teeth and gums the color of raw liver. He spoke in a hillman's twang. "May I be eternally damned if I have. Let's burn 'em where they stand."

Now Fargo spoke up for the first time since the trio had arrived. "You boys are mighty mistaken. Check our weapons—they ain't been fired recently. And look how tacky that blood is. These folks were killed sometime during the night."

"Don't blow smoke up my ass, woman killer," Iron Mike shot back. "You two killed them last night, all right. And you raped that woman and done for both the kids. But you couldn't see good enough to rob 'em thorough-like in the dark. So you come back this morning to finish the job."

"Yeah," green teeth pitched in, "and you cleaned your weapons afore you come back. Innocent as scrubbed angels, huh?"

"You boys seem to have it all worked out," Fargo said. "Real convenient-like. But you still got one big problem. Look at those bullet holes, and look at how that man's heart is practically blown clear out of his chest. Neither one of us has weapons with that large a caliber. But I notice you three have."

Iron Mike moved with surprising speed for such a big

man. He stepped closer and brought a vicious backhand across Fargo's lips, splitting them open.

"Iron Mike Scully takes no sass but sarsaparilla, mister. Who the hell are you?"

Fargo was not in the habit of giving information, only eliciting it from others.

"Look it up in the almanac," he replied.

"Every deck has its joker," Scully replied. This time he shot his ham-sized fist hard into Fargo's gut, doubling him up for at least ten seconds as he struggled to get his breath back.

"You got starch in your collar," Scully said. "I'll give you that much. Leroy," he called to Green Teeth, "this one rides the stallion. Go through his saddlebags and see if there's anything to identify him."

Iron Mike Scully tipped his head in McDougall's direction. "Why would a hard case like you be pards with a damn pasty-faced barber's clerk like him? Or is he your gal-boy?"

"According to your big idea, I raped the woman. So why would I need a gal-boy?"

"Christ Jesus!" Leroy called out from beside the Ovaro. "I found an army contract, boys. Buckskins here is an express rider for the army."

"You sure don't set up like no army messenger rider to me," Scully told Fargo. "I say both you jaspers are on the dodge. Fess up, mister. You two're range bums turned killer, uh?"

"Holy mother-lovin' shit!" Leroy added. "If you believe this here piece of paper, his name is Skye Fargo!"

"That s'pose to mean something?" Scully demanded. "I ain't never heard the name."

"I have," Romer, the ferret face, put in. "He's the drifter they call the Trailsman. He's been writ up big in the crap-sheets. They say he's left a trail of nameless graves from the Rio to the Tetons."

"That don't cut no ice with me," Scully said. "Them ink slingers are little old ladies of both sexes. These two cock-chafers have killed women and kids, and they *will* dance on air for it."

Scully pulled a smoker's bible from his vest pocket. He crimped a paper and shook some tobacco into it from a little sack, then quirled the ends and licked it. He lit a lucifer match on his tooth and fired up the smoke. When he looked at Fargo, his goading smile failed to include the corners of his mouth.

"All right, newspaper hero," he said, his voice caustic as acid, "where's the woman?"

Fargo nodded toward the dead woman. "Laying right there ten feet from you."

This earned Fargo several hard cuffs. "Bottle it, fucker!" Scully growled. "I'm talking about a younger woman. What did you do with her? You musta at least seen her."

"I ain't got the foggiest notion in hell what you're talking about," Fargo lied. "I rode in here only a few minutes before you three did."

"Quit taking me for a sleigh ride, Fargo. I asked if you seen a woman anywhere around here."

"He's telling the God's honest truth." Sitch spoke up. "I got here about ten minutes before Fargo. I didn't even know his name before you fellows brought it up."

"That's a lulu," Scully snapped. "Maybe you two birds will sing a little more when we fit both of you with a California collar."

"You're just gonna string us up?" Sitch protested. "No evidence, no lawyer, no nothing—just your say-so that we did it?"

"Oh, it'll be real legal-like," Leroy said, flashing his green teeth when he smirked. "You boys will get a miners' trial back at Rough and Ready. And, see, we won't exactly be stringing you *up*. 'Steada boosting you branchward, we'll toss the rope around your neck and then drag-hang you behind your own horses."

Fargo knew more than he cared to about the rope justice of territorial vigilantes and miners' courts. It would just be an occasion to get drunk before he and Sitch were murdered in cold blood in a deliberate travesty of justice. Fargo knew of one occasion where a mule was appointed counsel for the defense. This trail had taken a mighty ominous turn, and unless they could pull a rabbit out of a hat, Fargo could see no way to wangle out of this mess.

"Speaking of horses," Romer said, admiring the Ovaro,

"that's one humdinger of a stallion, boys. Us three will have to draw lots for it."

"That sorrel ain't no slouch, neither," Leroy said.

"Never mind that shit right now," Iron Mike snapped. "Get them two horses necked together so these mad-dog killers can't make a break for it when we take 'em back to camp."

"I'm just a mite curious," Fargo cut in. "You three are claiming to be outraged by this crime, but you aren't even going to make sure these folks are buried?"

"*Now* you're a Christian, huh?" Scully retorted. "But since you brought it up—you two killed 'em, so you'll bury 'em right now. But try just one parlor trick, Fargo, and you two will end up as buzzard shit."

The silver-mining camp called Rough and Ready was a tented berg of the type Fargo had seen dotting the Far West. It sprawled out fanwise from the dilapidated headframe of the mine. These men were not gravel-pan prospectors working independently—silver ore had to be mined from veins in the earth, and this group had formed a profit-sharing cooperative.

Fargo had heard, however, that so far there was damn little profit to share, and the ragtag appearance of the miners and their camp suggested that their rags-to-riches dream was far more rags than riches.

And just as Fargo had suspected, the miners' trial, held that evening when the workday was finished, was just another kangaroo court of the type typifying the western frontier. Iron Mike Scully acted as both prosecutor and judge, and the dozen or so red sashes flanking him put the brakes on any real dissent from the sixty or so assembled miners—especially since the red sashes toted the most formidable weapons in camp.

"There you got it, boys!" Iron Mike shouted after summing up his version of events. "We caught these two skunk-bit coyotes red-handed robbing the corpses. This bearded buckaroo here actually had the nerve to put his crimes on me, Romer and Leroy. The hog-stupid son of a bitch had no idea that all of us here in camp were the ones who sent for Clement Hightower to give us a hand. Now him and his whole family have gone to glory, thanks to these two murderers!"

At this intelligence, Fargo and Sitch exchanged a surprised glance. Scully and his two lickspittles had said nothing about this earlier.

The two prisoners were trussed tightly to adjacent trees, and Scully had deliberately selected a spot pockmarked with ant beds. Unable to slap at the pests, both men were plagued by the fiery bites.

"Hold on here a minute, Iron Mike," spoke up a tentative voice from the shadows.

A bonfire was burning in the middle of camp, casting lurid orange-yellow light on the assembled faces. Fargo watched a miner step forward into the brighter illumination. The Trailsman took in a slump-shouldered man with a strong hawk nose and a face lined deep like cracked leather. He looked vaguely familiar. But when Fargo spotted the nervous tic that kept the man's left eye winking half shut, he immediately recognized him.

"I know him," Fargo muttered to Sitch. "His name's Duffy Beckman."

"Well, you got a chicken bone caught in your throat?" Iron Mike demanded. "You got something to say, spit it out."

"It's just . . . Well, see, I know Skye Fargo, Mike. There ain't no way in pluperfect hell he coulda done what you're saying."

"You calling me a liar, Beckman?"

"'Course not," Duffy hastened to say. "I just think you're honestly mistaken. See, I was out at the prospecting camp called Buckskin Joe, back in the Rockies, when Fargo led us in a fight against claim jumpers. Sure, he's a killer when he's pushed to it and a damn good one. But he *ain't* no goldang murderer, most especial of women and kids."

"You like him, do you?"

"Well, I'm just saying he's a plumb good sort, is all."

Iron Mike gave a snort of derision. "Well, now, boys, sounds like the winker here is in love. We best get him to a whore in Carson City quick."

Plenty of men laughed at this, but Fargo noticed that others held silent. Now another voice spoke up from the flickering shadows.

"I ain't never met Fargo, Iron Mike. But I've heard this

and that about him. I never heard of no stain on his name. Might be we should slow down here, maybe poke into this thing a little more."

"Balls! I'm telling you flat-out we caught the son of a bitch picking over the bodies! Boys, plenty of men got them a newspaper reputation as 'heroes,' but them weak sisters in the newspaper trade are turning shit into strawberries on account it sells more papers. Duffy claims Fargo helped put the kibosh on some claim jumpers and maybe he did. But Duffy also admits Fargo's a killer and a damn good one."

Now Romer pitched into the game. "Boys, you didn't see it like me and Mike and Leroy done. That pretty woman and her innocent little girls, layin' there in the dirt like so much tossed-out trash! Women and little girls! Christ Almighty! Has it come to this—Western men defending the murderers of women and kids?"

This stirred the men up, and Iron Mike immediately took advantage of their strong emotions.

"Let's put it to the vote right now! All in favor of standing up for women and kids, sound off now!"

A loud chorus of assenting votes rose from the assembled miners.

"All who are opposed sound off!"

Fargo heard a few halfhearted no votes.

"That cinches it!" Iron Mike shouted triumphantly. "Tomorrow, just after sunup, we drag-hang these bastards."

The meeting broke up and Scully crossed toward Fargo. He brought a hard straight-arm punch into Fargo's already bruised and swollen lips, slamming his head back into the tree.

"You heard it, Fargo. You two galoots will see your last sunrise tomorrow. How you like *them* apples, hero?"

Fargo tasted salt as the blood pooled in his mouth. "Not too much," he admitted.

Iron Mike laughed before strolling away. Fargo had survived every manner of danger during his life on the frontier, including other seemingly hopeless situations where lesser men would have given up. But he didn't believe in miracles, and no matter how he sliced it, it seemed inevitable that tomorrow would indeed be his last glimpse of the sun.

3

"So you're Skye Fargo?" Sitch McDougall said when the two tightly trussed men were alone. "The hombre the ink slingers call the savage angel?"

"Looks like I'm soon to be the *late* Skye Fargo. I wouldn't mind it so much if I'd had me a woman recently. I hate like hell to die horny."

"*Damn* these ants!" Sitch complained. "Say, speaking of women—why did that greasy-haired bastard Scully ask you about one earlier?"

"That's got me treed," Fargo said. "But he wasn't just shooting at rovers—I did see a woman, a real looker, too, though I only caught a glance of her. Spotted her just about a couple hundred yards from the massacre site, hiding in the boulders. Her dress was covered with blood, so I'm figuring she must have escaped in the dark."

"Hunh. Didja talk to her?"

"You might say that. But the conversation was cut short when she took a shot at me."

"I thought I heard a shot, but I was still numb from what I was seeing."

"She took off running, and I'm hoping she followed my advice and went to Carson City. Otherwise, she won't have a snowball's chance of surviving."

Sitch cursed the ants again. "Fargo, I've come across my share of cutthroat bastards since I joined Dr. Geary's medicine show in Saint Louis and headed west. But this bunch under Scully could scare the devil out of hell."

"Yeah, they're a sweet outfit, all right. Did you notice that ferret face wears a human ear as a watch charm?"

"I wondered what that wrinkled piece of leather was."

It was autumn and a sudden moaning gust of cold wind added to Fargo's misery. A raft of clouds sent dark moon shadows sliding across Carson Valley. For several minutes both men were alone with their gloomy thoughts. Then:

"Fargo?"

"Yeah?"

"With our final reckoning coming in the morning, you think we should . . . you know, pray or something? I got plenty of sins on my head."

"If you were Bible-raised, go right ahead. I'm just a heathen."

"Think they'll at least bury us?"

Fargo grunted. "Sure, when the world grows honest. Face it, Sitch—unless we somehow escape, Scully is right. We'll end up as buzzard shit."

"Thanks for gilding the lily," Sitch replied sarcastically.

"Don't ask the question if you can't stomach the answer. I'm no sunshine peddler."

"It's prob'ly for the best anyhow. Burying me would likely just put me six feet closer to hell."

A few more minutes passed in gloomy silence. Fargo's ropes were so tight that he could barely even flex his muscles, and the ants were playing hell with him, their bites like fiery pinpoints. At least the late-night chill dulled the painful bites somewhat.

"*Can* we somehow escape?" Sitch asked in a tone laced with desperation.

"I'm cogitating on that, old son. So far I've come up with nothing but the sniffles."

"I read a nickel novel once called *Skye Fargo, Indian Slayer*. In that one, you escaped the jaws of death over and over. You even escaped from a tipi surrounded by dozens of armed Apaches—you tunneled out with your bare hands. Did that really happen?"

Fargo shook his head in disgust. "Hell, Sitch, you won't find Apaches living in a tipi—they sleep in wickiups or jacals or mostly in caves or behind stone windbreaks because they're usually on the run. That oughta tell you how much these word merchants know."

Fargo fell silent, noticing a shadow moving slowly toward

the two prisoners. Perhaps Scully was returning to play a little more thump-thump while he still had the chance.

The shadow took on human form as the clouds blew away from the full moon, and Fargo recognized Duffy Beckman with Fargo's Arkansas toothpick in his left hand. His right hand held the Henry, and Fargo's gun belt was draped over his shoulder. McDougall's harmonica pistol was tucked into his belt.

Maybe there *are* miracles, Fargo thought, hope surging within him.

Without saying a word, Duffy grounded all the weapons except the razor-honed toothpick. He made short work of cutting both men free. They briskly rubbed their arms and legs to restore normal circulation. Then Fargo buckled on his gun belt, tucked the Arkansas toothpick into its boot sheath and picked up the Henry—he welcomed its reassuring weight in his hand.

"Your horses are over in the rope corral," Duffy whispered. "I've already tacked them."

"Duffy," Fargo whispered back as all three men headed toward the corral on cat feet, "I ain't got the words. But you can't hang around here after this. You spoke up for me, and they'll put the crusher on you."

"I *ain't* hanging around," he replied. "My horse is tacked, too."

The Ovaro whiffled softly, greeting Fargo by pushing his nose into his chest. Fargo booted his long gun and stuck his foot into the stirrup. He was about to step up and over when disaster struck: one of the other horses, spooked by the sudden proximity of men whose smell it didn't recognize, rose up on its hind legs, neighing loudly.

This set the rest of the horses off, and within seconds the unholy racket had raised a shout of alarm in the camp.

Fargo cursed but reacted swiftly. He snatched his knife back out and slashed through the rope holding the horses in.

"Hi-*ya*!" he shouted, unlimbering his Colt and firing several shots into the air. "Hi-ya, hii-*ya*!"

The rataplan of hooves reverberated through the night as the mounts scattered in every direction. But by the time the men had mounted and calmed their own nervous horses, a withering fusillade of gunfire erupted from the camp as the miners hurried toward the corral.

"Make it hot for 'em!" Fargo shouted as bullets snapped past his ears with a blowfly drone.

He tugged his Henry from its saddle scabbard, tossed the butt plate into his shoulder socket, and started working the lever rapidly, aiming toward the approaching muzzle flashes. Sitch fired his cumbersome harmonica pistol as rapidly as he could, and Duffy made his long Jennings rifle sing. First one, then a second miner cried out in anguish as they were struck, and the advance halted as the miners sought cover.

Fargo led the desperate escape, heading west toward the forested foothills of the Sierra Nevada. A chance bullet caught his hat and spun it off his head, but Fargo caught it in midair. The three riders disappeared into the moonlit night, and despite being a heathen, Fargo felt the indescribable relief of a damned soul escaping from hell.

Fargo always tried to avoid riding after dark, especially at a good clip. Horses were most vulnerable in their long, slender legs, and rocks that were easily avoided in daylight could permanently cripple a horse at night. Knowing the red sashes wouldn't likely retrieve their mounts until well after daylight, he reined in at a tree-sheltered hollow only about four miles west of Rough and Ready.

"Hell," Sitch McDougall protested, "we just made a hot bustout with the odds against us a million to one. Why'n't we just keep on going while our horses are fresh? If we stay in these parts, we'll just be sticking our heads in a noose."

"Who died and made you boss?" Fargo retorted as he dismounted and began to pull his saddle.

"But—"

"But me no buts, card cheat. Do as you please. We ain't joined at the hip. I'm aiming to settle some scores and get some questions answered. You think I'm gonna let some blowhard son of a bitch beat the dog shit out of me, railroad me to a hanging and then just walk away from it?"

"Seems to me a sane man would be grateful just to be alive."

"Or a coward," Fargo said in a pointed tone. He turned to Duffy, faintly visible in the silver-white moonlight.

"Duffy, you saved our bacon, and I for one am beholden. I won't forget this."

"Skye, you saved plenty of us back at Buckskin Joe when that scum bucket Ike Perry turned his rented thugs on us. 'Sides, you two actually done me a favor by prodding me into action. For months now I been meaning to light a shuck for the gold camps still showing color in the Sierra."

"Slim pickings at Rough and Ready?"

Duffy was busy ground-tethering his coyote dun gelding. "Well, there's that. All of us are just barely making enough to keep the wolf from the door—not that we got a door."

"It's not usual," Fargo said, "for miners to stick so long where there's no profits."

"Well, see, we had what you might call an enticement. There's been this rumor, for a long time now, that there's a rich vein of silver somewheres around Rough and Ready."

"Yeah, I've heard that, too. Hell, Duffy, you know you can't set stock in mining-camp rumors," Fargo said as he began rubbing the Ovaro down with an old feed sack. "Look how Coronado and the rest of those dons listened to some scuttlebutt from Indians and wasted their lives searching for El Dorado."

"This ain't just the usual bubbling hearsay, Skye. That fellow you and McDougall found slaughtered—Clement Hightower. He's a college-trained mining engineer. He swears there's a fortune in that vein."

"Well, college trained or no, he could still be full of sheep dip."

"I s'pose. But, Skye, these young mining engineers today are pretty sharp."

"That's true," Fargo conceded. "I met a couple of them up on the Comstock, and they know their oats. But if he knows about a fortune in silver, why didn't he mine it?"

"On account he ran out of money and couldn't find any backers. But he has—well, *had*—him a family out in Oregon and had to get home and take care of them. A while back he sent a letter to the *Territorial Enterprise*, a newspaper up in Virginia City. He swore he could find that silver if somebody would stake him."

"So you boys at Rough and Ready pooled your money and sent for him?"

"That we did. And now somebody has slaughtered him and his family."

Fargo mulled all of this for a minute.

"Duffy," he said, "can you think of any reason why Mike Scully and his toad-eaters would have wiped out Hightower and his family?"

"You think he did?"

"Well, I did think that, yeah. But it doesn't make sense if Hightower was the key to the mint."

"No, it don't," Duffy agreed. "But far as asking me if Scully is low enough to do it, hell yes. He's the main reason I decided to light a shuck to the Sierra. Him and the rest of the sashes has always been pricks. 'Bout a month ago, though, he started swaggerin' around and actin' all biggity, like he owned the whole damn camp."

"A month ago," Fargo repeated. "Was that after you fellas wrote to Hightower?"

"Yep."

"Interesting," Fargo said.

"Look, Duffy," Sitch cut in, "I can't tell you how much I appreciate what you did for me and Fargo. And you've got the right idea—get the hell out of here before Scully and his minions do the hurt dance on you. But, Fargo, you're just looking for your own grave if you hang around here. Why not just return to your express rider job and leave this thing alone?"

"Mind your own beeswax," Fargo snapped. "That fine-looking sorrel you're riding—you boosted it, didn't you?"

"From a livery in Virginia City," Sitch admitted. "But, Christ, I had four pissed-off gamblers looking to buck me out in smoke."

"Not only a card cheat but a damn horse thief. And I should take advice from a scut like you? Besides, you're forgetting something. Scully and his maggots are going to spread the word far and wide that the two of us murdered women and children. Sure, they ain't the law and it won't have any official weight. But this is the frontier, full of hotheads and hair-trigger idiots who thrive on Dame Rumor. Either we clear our names or we live in caves the rest of our born days."

Even in the grainy darkness, Fargo saw McDougall's shoulders slump. He plopped down on a log. "Hell, I didn't think of that. All right, deal me in, but you're calling the shots."

"I always call the shots," Fargo assured him, "and I'm damned if I'm dealing you in. You'd be as useful to me as tits on a boar hog."

Fargo turned to Duffy again. "Duffy, there's a woman who escaped the attack. Could Scully have known about her before that family was slaughtered?"

"He could have, sure, if Hightower mentioned her in his letter."

"You didn't read the letter?"

"I can't read, Skye, but it wouldn't a mattered nohow on account Scully got the letter in Carson City and didn't read it to nobody. He just told us the Hightower family was on their way out. We had to build a cabin for the bunch of them, so maybe Clement said who was coming."

Fargo nodded. At first he'd been damned near convinced Scully and his pack of rabid curs perpetrated that massacre. But based on everything Duffy had told him, it just didn't make sense.

"I don't know who that woman is," Fargo mused aloud, "but if she's alive, I have to locate her. She could bust this deal wide open. Well, we best turn in."

"Damn straight," Duffy said. "Tomorrow at first light I'm gonna light out full bore for the Sierra."

Fargo took some comfort in the proximity of the rugged Sierra Nevada. In places it rose to an altitude of twelve thousand feet, and Fargo knew that range so well he could elude any pursuers there if need be. But hiding among snowy peaks wouldn't clear his name or answer the perplexing questions gnawing at him.

"Where we gonna sleep?" McDougall complained.

Duffy was astounded. "Where? Ain't you never slept under the stars before?"

"Not outside. I had a nice comfortable pallet in the back of Dr. Geary's medicine wagon."

It wasn't too dark for Duffy and Fargo to exchange a quick glance.

"Tell you what," Fargo said, "we'll make you a Tucson bed."

McDougall's tone grew more hopeful. "Thanks! What's a Tucson bed?"

"You lay on your belly," Duffy explained, "and cover up with your back."

Fargo snorted and McDougall cursed. "That's about as funny as a rubber crutch," he groused.

It was definitely one of that day's lighter moments. But as Fargo softened up bed ground with his knife, he couldn't shake two images painted on the backs of his eyelids: one was of four slaughtered innocents lying in the dirt, shot full of holes.

The other was of a beautiful, ashen-faced, blood-spattered woman racing through the boulders, so frightened that she promised to kill herself if he tried to approach her.

4

The next morning, with the day's new sun still a pink blush on the eastern horizon, Fargo dug a fire pit.

"The tree cover is good," he told the other two men, "and they won't spot the smoke. I'm not letting you hit the trail, Duffy, without some hot chuck in your belly."

Fortunately the red sashes hadn't gotten around to emptying his saddlebags. Fargo pulled out his blue enameled coffeepot and filled it with water from a goatskin water bag kept lashed to his saddle horn. He tossed a handful of coffee beans in it to boil. Then he mixed cornmeal with water and formed little balls with it, tossing them onto the hot ashes to bake into corn dodgers.

"Where you headed to in the Sierra?" he asked Duffy.

"Place called Hat Creek in Modoc County. Most of the easy color has played out in California, and the hard-rock operations has moved in, running the gravel-pan sourdoughs out. But my cousin Jed says there's still some good nuggets in the stream beds thereabouts."

"You got any money?" Fargo asked him.

"Only about twelve dollars in Spanish coins, but you're welcome to it—"

"I don't want your money, you dunderhead." Fargo cut him off. "You'll need a better stake than that. Scully and his puke pails emptied my pockets, but they didn't get my secret stash."

Fargo dug into the sack of cornmeal and pulled out two double eagle gold shiners.

"Here's forty dollars," he said. "Prices will be high in a gold camp, but this might tide you until you pan some high assay. Sitch, pony up."

"Hell, Fargo, they emptied my pockets too, and—"

"Don't hand me that shit. I never met a grifter yet who didn't have money in his boots. Give. This man saved your life."

McDougall wore a pair of buffalo-skin boots with the hair inside. With considerable effort he pried one off and produced two half eagles. "Ten dollars is all I got, my hand to God. But you're welcome to it, Duffy."

"Those boots don't fit you very good," Fargo remarked. "Did you kill the man you stole them from?"

"That's a libel on me." Sitch bristled. "I've never killed a man in my life. I won them in a crap game in Cheyenne."

"With loaded dice, anh?"

Sitch struggled to get the boot back on. "I don't see no halo on you, Fargo."

"Oh, I've still got my quota of original sin," the Trailsman admitted. He looked at Duffy again.

"There's a sheriff in Carson City, right? You know anything about him?" Fargo asked.

"His name is Cyrus Vance, and believe it or not he's not your usual bribes-or-bullets lawman. He's middling honest. But he couldn't solve a one-piece puzzle. He's gettin' long in the tooth now, and mainly he just jugs drunks and naps in his own jail cell. The magistrate is crooked as cat shit, though. Any offense can be settled out of court for the right amount. If you don't pony up the amount he demands, you're found guilty."

"This Sheriff Vance—how's he feel about Scully and the red sashes?"

"He wouldn't piss in their ears if their brains was on fire. They bullyrag him every time they get to town, but Vance ain't got no deputies so there ain't squat he can do about it. Matter fact, most folks in town can't stomach them."

"Interesting," Fargo said, tugging at his short chin whiskers.

"You're not thinking about going into Carson City, are you?" Sitch asked. "Hell, you'd be a sitting duck."

"Carson City is where I sent the woman to, and she's the only witness to what happened night before last. And maybe she can answer a few more questions that are biting at me."

"It was dark, Fargo. It's likely she didn't see much."

"Dark with a full moon. Besides, there's a good chance she heard something."

"That rings right," Duffy agreed, picking his teeth with a twig. "But the sashes will likely try to get the town stirred up agin you by claiming you killed women and kids. Happens that don't work, they'll give you a lead bath."

"Far as stirring the town up against me, you just said the boardwalkers can't stomach them. They don't have a shred of proof, just their say-so. As to killing me, even in the territories it's a serious business to kill a deputy sheriff."

Sitch choked and spat out a mouthful of coffee. Duffy's shoulders began to shake as he laughed silently. "You, a deputy sheriff? Fargo, you're planning to stir up the shit agin, ain'tcha?"

Fargo assumed a look of cherubic innocence. "With me it's live and let live—until it's time to kill or be killed. I'm a lovable cuss. And speaking of lovable—Carson City is where the females are. I'm starting to get amorous thoughts when I spot a knothole."

"I do wish you luck, Skye," Duffy said, tossing out the dregs of Fargo's river-mud coffee. "But I best skedaddle. That bunch back at camp might soon have their horses rounded up. You boys best light a shuck, too—this place ain't that far from Rough and Ready."

"I doubt if those cockroaches could track a buffalo herd through a mud wallow," Fargo said. "Look, Duffy, after what Scully and his bootlicks did to me yesterday, I got my mind set on either killing them or running them off. Might be you could hang around these parts a bit, join up again with your pards at the camp."

Duffy shook his head, looking suddenly embarrassed. "See, Skye, it ain't just Scully and them that's put jackrabbits in my socks. There's . . . things happening in Carson Valley. Things that give me the fantods."

Fargo's brow wrinkled in puzzlement. "The hell you talking about, old son?"

"You heard about what happened in this valley back in fifty-eight, right? How Paiutes wiped out a preacher and a bunch of church missionaries bound from the Humboldt River to Old Sac?"

23

Fargo nodded. "Sure. It started that half-assed legend about how this is now the 'Valley of Death' for any white intruders. Some claptrap about how there's 'wandering dead' going around sucking the blood of the living in hopes they can come back to life. But, Duffy, you don't believe that foolishness?"

"I didn't when I come here, Skye. But now . . . I ain't so sure. I ain't the first to scat, neither. Plenty of other miners has pulled up stakes. But I ain't talking no more about it—it's bad cess."

Fargo knew that Duffy was stubborn as a rented mule, and he didn't try to press the matter. But it piqued his curiosity—clearly the topic had unstrung Duffy's nerves, and Fargo didn't know him to be a superstitious man.

Duffy tacked his horse. "I thank both you gents for the stake. Mayhap we'll meet down the trail somewheres."

"How 'bout a shot of bust-head for the road?" Sitch suggested, pulling a stirrup cup and a flask from a saddle pocket.

The three men shared a drink, and Duffy pointed his bridle west toward the towering ermine-capped peaks of the Sierra Nevada.

"So he believes this is a haunted valley," Sitch remarked. "He doesn't strike me as the type who goes in for spirit knockings and such."

"Hard to know about a man when it comes to such things," Fargo said, his crop-bearded face thoughtful. "A man can have enough guts to fill a smokehouse when it comes to facing real danger, but then shrivel up like fried bacon when he hears about ghosts and such. Well, this is where we part ways, Sitch. Where you headed?"

"I was hoping you'd change your mind about me siding you for a time."

"No soap. It's nothing personal—you're a likable enough cuss. But you got nothing but green on your antlers and you'd be a liability to me what with the job I've got ahead of me."

"I can be more useful than you might think, Fargo. I'm a master pickpocket, and I could sell a double bed to the Pope," he boasted. "Never underrate a good grifter."

"I don't have too many meetings with the Pope," Fargo

barbed as he tossed the blanket and pad on the Ovaro. "I suggest you quit while you're behind."

"I admit I'm no frontiersman like you, but I'm tougher than you give me credit for. I grew up an orphan in Manhattan's notorious Five Points area and ran with the gang called the Plug-uglies."

"An orphan, huh?" Fargo said as he tossed on his saddle and tightened the girth. "That's a tough break," he added, knowing something about that himself. "But I don't need a grifter. You cheat at cards and you steal horses—those are both killing offenses out west. A man can't trust your word or your actions."

"I admit that neither gospel nor gunpowder will put me on the straight and narrow. I refuse to live as a common wage slave—why, most men bust their humps for twelve hours a day just to earn a measly dollar. But I never rook widows, old folks or the poor—or any man I call my friend. And I call you a friend."

"No need to slop over," Fargo shot back sarcastically.

"All right—but look here, Fargo," McDougall hastened to add, opening a saddle pocket. "A man like me who's often on the dodge has to be mighty resourceful."

He pulled out an impressive array of fake beards and mustaches with a bottle of spirit gum to affix them, spectacles with clear glass, even a priest's collar.

"I'm a disguise artist, too. In two minutes I can change my appearance so you wouldn't even recognize me, even with this homely face of mine. Think how handy that could be if you needed a man to do some eavesdropping for you."

"Look," Fargo said impatiently, "I'm not a Pinkerton man. And I got no use for a damn pickpocket or cardsharp or disguise artist. Mostly I'm a one-man outfit. If a man has some skills I might use, maybe he'll do to take along. What I don't need is a boardwalker who'd starve and go naked without stores."

"Skills, huh?" Sitch repeated, reaching into the other saddle pocket. He pulled out the finest whip Fargo had ever seen. The hickory handle was inlaid with ivory and the buckskin lash dyed gold.

"That's an impressive whip," Fargo said, pulling a thin black Mexican cigar from his shirt pocket.

"Had it custom made for me in Saint Louis before I joined the traveling medicine show."

Fargo, still admiring the whip, pulled a lucifer match from his possibles bag. Before he could scratch it to life with a thumbnail, McDougall's whip cracked and the match burst into flame.

"Damn," Fargo said, astonished at such fine-tuned accuracy. "I guess you *are* a trick-whip expert."

But the demonstration wasn't over yet. The whip cracked again and Fargo's dusty white hat flew straight up off his head. With rapid, successive cracks, Sitch kept the hat aloft like a hovering hummingbird for at least ten seconds. To Fargo's utter amazement, Sitch dropped the hat back onto Fargo's head perfectly.

"Damn and double damn!" Fargo said in an amazed tone.

"Not all my tricks are just for show," Sitch assured him. Again the whip cracked, and Fargo's Colt was lifted from his holster and dropped on the ground about ten feet away. "Would you call *that* a useful skill?" he demanded.

"Sure as little green apples," Fargo admitted, retrieving his six-gun. "I've never seen any man handier with a whip. But I watched you shooting that harmonica pistol last night, and you were bucking that gun like a frightened schoolchild. And you've got a round ass in the saddle. You belong back in the land of steady habits working sideshows."

"And I suppose you were never green yourself, huh? Nobody ever taught you a thing about frontier survival, right? You just came out of the womb ready to kick ass and take names?"

McDougall's tone had turned from wheedling to bitterness. For a moment Fargo thought about the legendary mountain man Corey Webster, who had saved young Fargo's life in the days when the man who eventually became known as the Trailsman was still too green to survive a bad winter storm in the Rockies.

"I learned from my betters," Fargo conceded.

"Fargo, I'll tell you the straight truth—I'm scared. I was stupid and I had to flee from Virginia City and the medicine show. Now I'm on my own in godforsaken country, and I don't even know how to locate the North Star or hunt or read a trail. Hell, yesterday I didn't even have enough sense to notice that those hoofprints around that burning wagon were made by iron-shod horses. But I'm a damn quick study. If I could just side you for a bit, watch you and learn . . . I'm just trying to stay alive, that's all."

Fargo cursed silently because he felt himself giving in against his better judgment. He suspected Sitch McDougall would be nothing but a millstone around his neck, but Fargo had never once turned his back on a man making a desperate appeal for help.

"All right, damn it," he said gruffly. "But I *ain't* your damn sugar tit. I'll put up with you for a spell, but you can flush all that cheap-novel foolishness out of your headgear right now. Was it one of my 'miracle escapes' that saved our bacon last night?"

"Nope. It was Duffy Beckman."

"Right. I can be killed like any other man, and that means you die with me. We got a rough piece of work ahead of us, mister, and I'd wager you're going to regret you ever asked for a share of it. And one more thing . . ."

"Yeah?"

"Don't keep that whip in your saddlebag—put it behind your belt. It's your best weapon, and a weapon is useless if it isn't right to hand when you need it. And I guarandamntee— you *will* be needing it."

5

The two horsebackers bore southeast, Fargo leading them well away from the stage road to Carson City.

"Are you really serious about trying to become a deputy?" Sitch asked.

"Serious as a gutshot."

"But I read somewhere that you refuse to swear oaths?"

"I don't swear loyalty oaths to any government," Fargo corrected him. "Swearing to uphold the law is another matter."

"Yeah," Sitch persisted, "but do you really plan to uphold it?"

"Insofar as I can. Out here in the Territories you sometimes have to make up the law as you go along. Anyhow, this Sheriff Vance might just tell me to go to hell."

The terrain around them varied widely, often dominated by barrancas, ravines that sliced the land unevenly.

"Stop fighting that horse," Fargo ordered the frontier novice. "Give it its head when he wants it, let him sniff the ground. Horses need to do that in new territory so they can settle down. And don't sit so damn stiff on the saddle—sit *in* it, and learn to ease into the horse's gait or your ass will blister until you can't sit down."

"That woman you saw," Sitch remarked a few minutes later, "I wonder if she made it to Carson City. And I can't help wondering why Scully made it a point to press you about her."

"Same here," Fargo said. "All we can do is look for her. What I can't figure is who killed Clement Hightower and his family, and why. From what Duffy told us, it wouldn't make sense for the red sashes to do it. They needed him to find this big vein of silver, assuming there is one."

"Yeah, but they were sure in a puffing hurry to pin it on us. Seems to me that's what you'd do if you were eager to wash the blood off your own hands."

Fargo glanced at Sitch. "You're not stupid about everything, are you? I guess criminal minds think alike. And have you been wondering about this haunted valley deal and what it would take to scare miners so bad they just up and left like Duffy's doing?"

"You think it's all tied in?"

"I don't think it, but I wonder about it."

They rode for a few more minutes in silence, Fargo's sun-slitted eyes in constant motion.

"Here's a good one for you," Sitch said. "There's this little kid, see, and he's got this collie dog he loves to dickens. Well, that collie keeps wandering over to the neighboring farm and scattering the chickens all to hell. Finally the farmer gets sick of this and takes a shot at the dog.

"Well, the collie manages to crawl back home before it dies. The kid's madder than a wet hen and goes into town to fetch the sheriff back to look at the dog. The lawman stoops down and takes a good look at the wound. 'Hmm,' he says, 'rectum.' 'Wrecked him, hell!' the kid screams back. 'The son of a bitch killed him!'"

Sitch laughed with gusto at his own joke. Fargo's lips twitched in what might or might not have been a grin.

"Hell," Sitch protested, "that's a ripsnorter. You must not know what a rectum is."

"'Course I do. It's an asshole, and I'm riding beside one right now. Let me give you some unfriendly advice: keep your damn mouth shut and your eyes and ears open. You haven't looked behind you once since we set out from camp. *Always* keep a close eye on your backtrail, especially in country with hostile tribes. Duffy mentioned that attack on the church people back in fifty-eight, but just last year was the Battle of Pyramid Lake."

"What was that all about?"

"Paiutes killed almost eighty white men who got liquored up and decided to teach the Indians a lesson. They found out that you *don't* want to cross that tribe. Paiutes have got two favorite ways to kill a whiteskin: bury him alive or burn him alive. I like a good joke as much as the next fellow, but only when I'm in a safe place. You cried about how you want to learn to survive out here, so you best start learning."

"Point taken," Sitch said somberly. "I have been looking around me."

"Yeah, but when you're scouting open country you don't really want to *look* for anything special. Scan the wide view with your eyes focused to the middle distance, watching for movement or reflections, not shapes. Don't focus on anything special—just let the country sort of roll up to your eyes. It takes a while, but you'll get the hang of it."

"Have you seen any sign of the red sashes?"

"I'd say they're beating the bushes for us, all right. I've seen dust puffs made by horses, likely Scully and his grave-yard rats tossing a net out for us. Rein in for a minute."

Fargo removed his 7X army field glasses from a saddle pocket and took a closer look toward some of those puffs.

"Yeah, he's far out from us, but I can just make out Leroy. 'Member him, the one with the green teeth? We need to watch out for him—if he can use that Hawken rifle of his, he's trouble plenty. A Hawken is single-shot, but it's got twice the range of my Henry, and with that half-ounce ball it fires, even a hit to the arm will shock a man to death."

"Seems to me," Sitch remarked, "that some of them will be covering the approaches closer to Carson City, too."

"Now you're using your think piece. They'll likely make it hot for us."

Fargo relaxed somewhat when they entered a forested expanse of ponderosa pine. Soon they reached a clear, wide, sand-bottom creek. When McDougall started to ride into it, Fargo whistled him back.

"That's a soft sand bottom. Dismount and water your horse first before you ford. Otherwise it'll stop in the middle to drink and might become mired. A mired horse can panic and kill itself trying to get free."

"Man alive! I wish I could write all this down."

Fargo lit down, shaking his head in disgust. "I s'pose next you'll be wanting a hornbook and a quill? Write it down in your head, you fool."

Both men forded the creek and soon broke over a low rise

overlooking Carson City, still about a mile south but clearly visible. The problem was the wide-open expanse leading up to it.

"That big clutch of boulders on the left will be trouble," Fargo predicted. "Here's how we'll play this deal. I want you to ride out first. Hunker low in the saddle, bent over the horn, and thump that sorrel hard with your heels. Ki-yi him up to a headlong run. Make sure you keep your feet well into the stirrups because you'll be bouncing hard up on the hurricane deck."

"Why me first?"

"Because I'm the one they really want, and they'll recognize my Ovaro right off. I'll draw their fire off of you."

"Maybe they won't be there."

"I hope so," Fargo said, "but you don't stay alive in Zeb Pike's West by assuming the best. Now, make tracks and make 'em quick."

Fargo smacked the sorrel's glossy rump hard. "Hee-*yah!*"

The big seventeen-hand gelding shot off like an arrow from a bow. Fargo waited ten seconds, then speared his Henry from its boot and chambered a round. He pressured the Ovaro hard with his knees. The stallion, eager for a good run, laid back his ears and took off, quickly lengthening his stride.

At first, when no gunfire erupted, Fargo wondered if he had guessed wrong. But after about a quarter mile, a harsh hammering of gunfire punctuated the rataplan of the Ovaro's thundering hooves. The first few rounds were ranging shots; then the ambushers quickly got more accurate as they found their effective distance. One round passed so close to Fargo's face he felt the wind-rip from it.

Hanging on with his legs, Fargo took the reins in his teeth and swiveled slightly left in the saddle, setting the Henry into his shoulder socket. He could see gray-white powder smoke hazing the spot where the shooters had hidden among the boulders.

Now the Henry's sixteen-round magazine became crucial as Fargo levered and fired, levered and fired, setting up a steady whine of ricochets as his bullets splatted into the boulders. He knew from grim experience that steady ricochets could be just as deadly as direct fire and even more unnerving. And his tactic proved a good one as the dry-gulchers suddenly ceased fire. Moments later Fargo heard the drumbeat of escaping hooves.

Sitch McDougall, his face pale as new linen, waited for Fargo just past the edge of town. "Christ, they'd've turned you into a sieve if you hadn't scared them off. I just can't figure out why they're so bent on killing us—or at least you. Is it because they fear you'll turn the suspicion for that massacre on them?"

"That's a poser," Fargo replied. "I don't believe for one damn minute that bunch of demented jackals care a frog's fat ass about that family. But they sure care about something, and I aim to find out what it is."

Fargo waited a minute to let the Henry's long barrel cool down a bit before dropping it back into his saddle scabbard.

"Well, we've met the welcoming committee," he said, gigging the Ovaro forward. "Now let's go meet the sheriff."

Carson City, capital of the newly organized Nevada Territory, was a thriving boomtown with no bust in sight. It had become the main outfitting center for the Comstock Lode just to the north, where silver and gold strikes had produced millionaires who possessed more money than the entire U.S. Treasury. Fargo had passed through Carson City before and knew that half the population were floaters, many of them gamblers who kept a horse saddled close by.

The impressive main street boasted solid buildings with raw-lumber false fronts and new boardwalks. It was also so thick with human and animal traffic that no one bothered to notice the two new arrivals as they trotted into town.

"Jesus," Sitch remarked, "are those men lying in front of the saloons dead?"

"Just drunks tossed outside to sleep it off," Fargo replied. "If they had any money when they were thrown out, they won't have it when they wake up."

Several of the usual town loafers occupied a pine bench in front of the sheriff's office, whittling and swapping lies. They scrutinized the two riders as they reined in and tied off at the snorting post.

"Hey, buckskins," one old codger called out, "where you settin' your beaver traps—out in the desert?"

"Best keep your mouth closed, Methuselah," Fargo called back, "or those wooden teeth will fall out."

The two men strolled inside, and the first thing Fargo spotted was a sign on the back wall over the two empty jail cells:

NEVER DO ANYTHING WRONG—WHEN SOMEBODY'S LOOKING.

"Help you, gents?" said a man seated behind a kneehole desk and drinking a glass of milk.

"Sheriff Vance?" Fargo asked.

"Ever since birth. And who's inquiring?"

"My name is Fargo. This homely plug with me is Mitt McDougall."

"Fargo, is it? Would that be Skye Fargo, the jasper they call the Trailsman?"

Fargo nodded, and the sheriff sat up a little straighter in his chair. Sheriff Cyrus Vance was thickset without running to fat, his rumpled hair shot through with streaks of silver. He had a weather-grooved face and tired eyes like raw wounds. A watery nose made him sniff constantly.

"Well I'll be hog-tied and earmarked. . . . I heard all that shooting outside of town a few minutes ago. Bein's who you are, I take it you know something about it?"

"Unfortunately, yes. That's why we're here."

"Pull up them two chairs, boys, and take a load off. I got the feeling this is going to be quite a story."

Fargo started at the beginning, the discovery of the massacred family a few miles north of the mining camp at Rough and Ready. He described the summary arrest and "trial" at the hands of the red sashes, the escape thanks to Duffy Beckman and the ambush just now.

"So you boys tangled with Iron Mike Scully and his hyenas?" the sheriff remarked when Fargo had finished. "I don't care shucks for the son of a buck, but he's a potent force to be reckoned with. He's two hundred pounds of hard, and them two fancy-grip Navy Colts of his ain't just for show—he can draw so quick that he's a day younger when he shoots."

Sitch's brow furrowed in confusion. "I don't get that one," he put in.

The sheriff glanced at him and sniffed, then took a swig of his milk. "It's just a manner of speaking, son. You know, you look a lot like a description I got yesterday of a horse thief up in Virginia City."

"All ugly men look alike, Sheriff. Besides, every man breaks the law if you follow him long enough."

Vance grinned. "Ain't that the Gospel truth? But, say, did you steal that horse? It's a big sorrel with two front white socks."

"I did," Sitch fessed up boldly, startling Fargo and the sheriff. "It's tied off out front right now."

"Well, Jesus! You don't just swagger in to a sheriff's office and brag about horse stealing. What kind of respect does that show my badge?"

"Would it be more respectful, Sheriff, to lie to your face about it? Besides, it was a matter of life and death. There was a . . . mishap at a gambling table, and I was forced to exert myself in retreat or die of lead colic."

The sheriff stared at Fargo. "You know, Trailsman, a man is judged by the company he keeps. I've always had a good impression of you despite the fact that you've busted a few lawmen in the chops over the years."

"You might call this half-wit my hair shirt," Fargo replied. "I'd be grateful if you lock him up for the crime he just confessed to."

The sheriff mulled this for about fifteen seconds, sipping more milk. Then he stared at Sitch. "Well, since you're with Fargo, and I don't want to see you hang . . . but I didn't hear anything you said about that horse, y'unnerstan'? And you best mind your pints and quarts in my town, savvy?"

Sitch pointed his chin toward the sign. "I will—when somebody's looking."

"Don't push your luck," Fargo snapped, regretful that Vance hadn't at least collared McDougall and tossed him into the calaboose for a time to teach him a lesson.

Vance turned his attention to Fargo again. "Yeah, I just started a report about that massacre—one of the silver miners brought me word of it, and I'm planning to ride out there and poke around a little before I submit it. It'll go nowhere, though, even with women and kids killed. We got a magistrate here in town, and a circuit judge rides in once a month. But there were no witnesses. Anyhow, don't worry about Scully and that bunch accusing you—their word ain't worth a busted trace chain."

There was one witness, all right, Fargo told himself—one covered with blood. But some instinct told him to keep that dark from the sheriff. However, the canny old bird seemed to read something in Fargo's face.

"You ain't being cute on me, are you? Holding something back?"

"Not a thing," Fargo lied effortlessly. "But I hope to turn something up."

This was the perfect moment to bring up the issue of swearing Fargo in as a deputy, but Fargo sensed the time wasn't right.

"This blasted valley," the sheriff complained. "I'm commencing to wonder if it *is* haunted, after all—or at least cursed."

He drank some more milk, his face wrinkling at the taste.

"You don't seem to enjoy that very much," Fargo noted.

"I druther drink horse piss. But thank the Lord we got a few milk cows around here."

"Stomach problems?"

"I'll tell the world. Back in the forties I joined up with the Texas Rangers. I passed the shooting and riding tests with flying colors. But you know what finally done me in? Bad digestion. Those old boys ride hard for days straight, sometimes living on hardtack or even piñon nuts. My stomach just gave out on me, and it's got worse since."

Fargo, who had a cast-iron stomach himself, was sympathetic. A man with weak digestion was better off in town. He knew of prospectors who had died of stomach ailments rather than give up their claims.

Vance nodded toward the milk. "I have to drink five, six glasses a day just to keep the burning down. Bad food has killed more men out west than six-guns have."

The sheriff suddenly recalled something Fargo had said earlier. "Wha'd'you mean, you hope to turn something up?"

This, Fargo realized, was the perfect opening.

"Sheriff, me and McDougall here buried those four bodies. The woman was raped, and her and those two little girls were shot up so bad they looked like targets at a turkey shoot. Something stinks bad here, and those red sashes are mixed up in it."

"You think they did it?"

"I can't say that—yet. But they seem awful damn eager to kill me, and I can't see the point of it. Trouble is, I've got no authority to do much about it, especially since you're the sheriff hereabouts. So I'm wondering—would you consider swearing me in as a temporary deputy?"

Vance hadn't expected anything like this. He rubbed his chin, conning it over.

"Well, I don't rightly know . . . For one thing, I got no funds to hire a deputy."

"An unpaid deputy," Fargo clarified even though he and McDougall were both flat broke.

"Hmm . . . I gotta admit it would be a novelty to have the Trailsman packing a star here in Carson City. But, say, you ain't just aiming to use a badge to settle some scores against Scully, are you?"

"Nope. I have a score to settle with him, all right, but I don't require a badge to do that. But I think there's a lot more to this deal, and I think it might help me find out about it if I'm a lawman."

Vance was warming up to the idea. "There's nothing I'd like better than to see the killers of women and kids brought to account. But, Fargo, if you're a badge toter, you can't just ignore everything else to work one crime. You'd be expected to enforce the law, period. Leastways, the ones that truly need enforcing."

Fargo nodded. "That's jake by me."

"You don't expect me to swear this horse thief in, too, do you?"

Fargo grunted. "He's likely the first jasper I'll arrest."

"All right, we'll forget the raise-the-right-hand business. Consider yourself sworn in. You can wear my old badge."

Vance banged open a desk drawer and tossed Fargo a badly tarnished tin star. Fargo pinned it to his shirt.

"I can snitch enough out of the municipal fund," the law-man said, "so's you boys can get your eats and have a little pocket money."

"'Preciate that," Fargo said.

"You'll find the usual riffraff in town," Sheriff Vance explained, "but very few gunslingers. Most of our trouble is armed robberies, not killings. Carson City is a favorite hoo-rah town for high-Sierra prospectors on a weekend bender. An ounce of gold dust fetches between fifteen and eighteen dollars, and most of those lunkheads carry their entire fortune with them."

He sent a pointed glance toward Sitch. "And we get the usual share of gambling shoot-ups. You best keep that in mind before you mark the aces."

He looked at Fargo again. "I hear you're a tomcat on the prowl?"

"I enjoy the fair sex," Fargo said from a deadpan face.

Vance snorted. "Yeah, well, there's six watering holes in town, but the Sawdust Corner is the cleanest and most popular. That's your best bet for . . . enjoying the fair sex. They got some pretty dime-a-dance gals, a fair-to-middling piano player, and a string of whores topside."

The sheriff swigged from his milk again and muttered a curse. "Avoid the faro game there—it's rigged. But they don't baptize their liquor, and if you spend eight bits or more you can eat at the free-lunch counter. There's not usually too much ruckus there unless that vigilante trash from Rough and Ready comes to town. The other miners ain't so bad."

He pointed toward a wooden file cabinet in the rear corner. "That's where I keep the reward dodgers. Mostly I use 'em for kindling, but go through them now and again. You two got a place to bed down?"

"We just now rode into town," Fargo said.

"Well, there's Ma Kunkle's boardinghouse. It's that big, knocked-together frame building just past the feed stable. Or you're welcome to sleep in the cells if they're empty."

"Given this bunch from Rough and Ready, I'd prefer to camp just outside of town at night. I'll tell you where I am in case you need me."

"We could use a bathhouse, though," Sitch said.

"Yeah, you sure could—you're both a mite whiffy. There's a Chinee bathhouse right next to the Sawdust Corner."

Both men were headed toward the door when Sheriff Vance called out Fargo's name. He turned around.

"I know your reputation, Trailsman, and the first second I laid eyes on you I knew you're a man I wouldn't want to cross. But for God's sake, son, *don't* underrate Iron Mike Scully. A few men have made that mistake, and not one even cleared leather before he popped them over."

6

There was a ramshackle feed stable on the western edge of Carson City. As the two men headed in that direction, Sitch said, "You know, that old skinflint could've given us some of that pocket money he mentioned. We're both so broke, we can't even pay attention."

"You don't deserve one red cent," Fargo pointed out. "I'm the one working for no pay."

"You know, I've got half a mind—"

"At most," Fargo interposed.

Sitch shot him a reproving glance. "Oh, I get it—jokes are just fine when you tell them?"

"Who's joking?"

"Well, anyhow, like I was saying, I've got half a mind to scare up a friendly game of chance. Even without cheating I'm good at draw poker."

"Nix on that. In the first place, you'd need money to deal yourself in. And in the second place, a poker cheat never reforms. You just steer clear of the baize tables, and that's an order."

"Damn! Five minutes a deputy and you're already swinging your eggs."

"You said earlier I was calling the shots, remember? I'm letting you string along with me against my better judgment. You don't like my terms, head for the horizon."

"Your terms are just fine. Forget I said anything."

The two men turned into a big, hoof-packed yard in front of the livery. A young livery boy was perched on the top rail of the paddock plaiting a horsehair rope.

"You work here, son?" Fargo called out as he swung down.

"Yessir. Man alive, that's a fine-looking stallion."

Fargo slipped the bit and loosened the cinch. "How 'bout you give both these horses a rubdown and a curry, then grain them?"

"Sure."

"That sorrel gelding is gentle, but let my horse get a good smell of you first before you get behind him. He's been known to kick. You got a boss inside?"

"Yessir, Mr. Peatross. He's in there somewheres."

"How we gonna pay for this?" Sitch asked as the two men strolled toward the big barn.

"I think I know a way we can settle up just for today. We won't really have to grain these horses once we start camping outside of town where they can graze nights. These dry autumns in Nevada gradually dry and cure the grass like hay. Horses thrive on it. Tell you the truth I really just want to talk to the hostler. Nobody else, except maybe the soiled doves, knows more about what's going on around a town."

The inside of the barn was dim and fragrant with the smell of hay, horse manure, liniment and leather. They found the hostler inside the tack room using saddle soap to soften a big aparejo, a pack saddle designed in the Southwest.

"You Peatross?" Fargo inquired.

"I been called worse," Peatross replied. He was an old salt with a grizzle-bearded face, wrinkled as a peach pit and skin sagging off his bones. He squinted in the dim light, catching sight of the badge pinned to Fargo's shirt. "Lawman passing through, huh?"

"Nope. Sheriff Vance just put me on as a deputy."

"Vance," Peatross repeated sarcastically. "Always belly-achin' about his belly aching. I swan, if Ma Kunkle's milk cow ever dries up, that man will have to move to dairy country."

The old-timer studied Fargo more closely. "You set up pretty good, mister. You sure don't look like the soft-handed town type."

His rheumy gaze shifted to Sitch. "You," he said bluntly, "look like the type who'd steal a hot stove and sneak back for the smoke. What's the deal with that fancy whip in your belt? Steal it?"

"See that spider on the beam beside you?" Sitch said, pulling the whip out. He cracked the popper and turned the spider into a grease spot.

"Holy Hannah," Peatross said. "I know a mule from a burro, and I reckon I'll cinch my lips before you snap my nose off."

"Here's the deal," Fargo said. "Right now both of us are light in the pockets."

"I suspicioned that when I caught the stench blowin' off you."

"You've seen the whip," Fargo added. "Would it be worth a few dollars as collateral just until I can squeeze some money out of the sheriff?"

"Now, hold on, Fargo," Sitch objected. "You yourself said it was my best weapon and I should keep it to hand."

"Fargo?" Peatross repeated. "That wouldn't be Skye Fargo, would it?"

"That's him," Sitch said. "The hero of the penny dreadfuls and the Romeo of the range."

"Something mighty consequential is going on around here," the hostler announced, "if Skye Fargo has pinned on a badge. Well, forget about the whip. Would five dollars help you out, Fargo? I trust you for it."

"I appreciate the hell right out of that, Mr. Peatross," Fargo said. "I'll make sure you get it back."

The old man opened a tin cash box and handed the Trailsman a five-dollar shiner. The kid led the horses in, and the old codger crossed closer to inspect Fargo's stallion.

"That's the Ovaro, all right," he said. "Mighty fine horseflesh."

However, Peatross still didn't trust Fargo's companion. He checked the sorrel's flanks carefully for a brand. Fortunately for Sitch, the gelding's rightful owner hadn't branded it.

"I got a question," Fargo said. "I been hearing a lot of claptrap about how Carson Valley is haunted. What's the deal with that?"

"Claptrap, huh? Listen here, Deputy Fargo, if I was a younger man I'd clear out of these parts. There *is* a hoodoo on this valley, and that's straight arrow."

"What do you mean, 'hoodoo'?"

"The dead are walking and sucking blood, that's what I mean. I seen one of the corpses my own self when they fetched it to town—a drummer killed just a mile from Rough and Ready. Bit through the jugular, he was, just two fang marks. And that poor soul was drained so white he looked like he was leeched—mister, I mean white as a fish belly. Damnedest thing I ever seen."

Fargo figured the old man was so full of shit, his feet were sliding. But after all, he had just lent the Trailsman five dollars, so Fargo kept his tone respectful.

"Yeah, that would make a man wonder. Maybe he was just snakebit."

"A snake what sucked him dry of blood? Horse apples! And that ain't all. Lotsa folks hereabouts, me included, has seen these queer, colored lights driftin' out over the valley at night. And there's bloodcurdlin' screeches like souls in torment, and folks has been—whatchacallit—accosted by the most fearsome creatures. So fry *them* tomatoes, deputy."

"No need to have a hissy fit, old roadster. I didn't mean to ruffle your feathers. I was just curious, is all."

"Well, it would sound a mite queer to an outlander. But if you stick around the valley long enough, you'll likely become a believer."

Fargo thanked Peatross again for the loan, and he and Sitch hoofed it toward the bathhouse.

"Damn, Fargo," Sitch opined, "that's Duffy, the sheriff and old Peatross who believe this area is spooked."

"Sheriff Vance didn't actually say he believes it," Fargo gainsaid. "And the whole thing is a crock of shit. But somebody is sure's hell working mighty hard to convince these folks—and I got a hunch it's the miners they're looking to drive out, not the townies. I just can't help thinking it's somehow tied into what happened to the Hightower family—and maybe into this sudden interest the red sashes have in sending me under."

Even when soaking in a tub of hot, sudsy water Fargo kept his weapons within reach and never took his eyes off the curtained doorway leading into the bathhouse.

"This is more like it," Sitch said from the tub beside him.

"You have to admit, Fargo, towns have some advantages over the high lonesome."

"I admit it," Fargo said. "A cold glass of beer, a poker game, a friendly woman, a box of ammo—towns got their uses. I've been to some big cities, though, that I wouldn't trade an old dog turd for."

"I like big cities. All the stirring and hullabaloo lifts my spirits."

"Bully for you."

"Well, you can't stop progress," Sitch insisted.

"There we agree. I don't try to stop it—I just try to avoid it."

"Oh yeah? I notice you carry a flint and steel in that little rawhide bag on your belt, but you light your cigars with matches."

"A match is just gunpowder on a stick, and gunpowder's been around for centuries. The 'progress' you're talking about will mostly benefit the rich at the expense of manhood and freedom. When the frontier is finally all mapped and settled, the New York land hunters and the railroad and mining barons will divvy it up amongst themselves. And the common men will turn against each other just to get some crumbs off their tables."

"I guess there's something to that," Sitch allowed. "The railroads east of the Missouri take all the land they want, and Congress kisses their asses and takes their bribes."

Fargo just grunted. This was no revelation to him. The two men finished their baths, dusted off their clothing and went back onto the street. By now it was well into the afternoon, the sun starting to throw long shadows.

"Well, now," Fargo remarked, glancing across the wide, dusty main street, "looks like we got us a guardian angel."

He had spotted a man wearing a red sash on his belt. His back was propped against the front of a mercantile, and he was obviously closely watching the Chinese bathhouse. He was not one of the three men who had taken Fargo and Sitch prisoner.

"Let's go pay our respects," Fargo suggested as he crossed the street.

The man turned and started to leave, but Fargo's long legs propelled him quickly onto the boardwalk, cutting the man off.

"I can't tell you how honored I am," Fargo greeted him, "to know you boys from Rough and Ready are watching over me."

"You're crazy as a loon. I was just resting for a spell."

Fargo smiled with his lips only, his penetrating, direct-as-searchlights eyes sending a different message. "Hogwash. Scully sent you to town to spy on me."

"Do tell?" the sash replied. He had the eyes of a sullen animal in a face that was all shrewd angles and planes. He did a double take when he noticed the star pinned to Fargo's buckskin shirt.

"I see you've tied down your holster," Fargo goaded. "I reckon you're about half rough, huh? One of those fearsome pistoleros?"

"Is there some law against a man tying his holster down?"

"Nope. You can tie it to your dick if you've a mind to. No law against watching a man from a public street, neither."

"Then how's come you're rousting me, *deputy*?"

Again Fargo smiled his mirthless smile. "Now that's mite unspiritual of you. I just came over to palaver with you. See, I always take a special interest in greasy bastards who try to lynch me. I'm eccentric that way."

"Lynch you? Good luck proving it in court."

The vigilante tried to brush past Fargo, but a grip on his gun arm like an eagle's talon trapped him.

"Tell me something, pistolero. Just why do you and your pals have such a keen interest in Skye Fargo?"

"Listen, Fargo, it ain't a smart idea to be playing cock of the dungheap around here. That tin star ain't worth a kiss-my-ass. Ask Sheriff Vance what happens to fools who try to buck Iron Mike Scully and his boys."

"Oh, I'll be killing Scully, all right," Fargo said in an amiable tone. "All in good time. But not before I find out what you sage rats are up to."

"You're off your chump. We ain't up to nothing. We just keep the peace out at the camp."

His hand moving swift as a striking snake, Fargo snatched the thug's Remington from its holster and handed it to Sitch. There was an alley at the corner of the mercantile, and before the red sash realized what was happening, Fargo had dragged him into it.

"Lissenup, Baron of Gray Matter," he said, dropping the amiable tone. "So far, I got nothing personal against you, and if you play your cards smart you might live. I don't go out of my way to fill new graves. But I don't like being spied on and lied to, and I'm giving you one last chance to spill the beans."

"Fuck you. And give me that gun back or you'll live to regret taking it."

Fargo nodded. "So that's your final word? Well, here's how it is: the next time I spot you around here, you'll be shoveling coal in hell. Sitch, keep an eye out for passersby."

Fargo drove a savage uppercut into the thug's chin, slamming his head back hard into the building. Next he drove a straight arm left into his sternum, then finished him off with a powerful roundhouse right. The vigilante collapsed into a heap as if his bones had suddenly gelled.

Fargo removed the man's gun belt. "Catch," he called to Sitch, flipping the belt to him. "Now you got a decent sidearm."

"All right, but isn't that outright theft?" said the unrepentant horse thief without a trace of irony.

"Now how could a man as young as you have such a shaky memory? You won that rig in a friendly game of chance, remember? I was there as a witness, and I'm a lawman, right?"

Sitch grinned and buckled on the gun belt, holstering the Remington. "Right as rain. Say, you didn't kill him, did you?"

"Nah," Fargo replied. "Dead men don't moan."

7

The new deputy and his disreputable companion found an eating house on one of Carson City's three cross streets and ordered beef and biscuits and big slabs of apple pie. Just before sunset they retrieved their horses and Fargo selected a campsite almost within hailing distance of the town, a little hollow ringed with boulders and with plenty of grass for the horses to graze.

He rode back to the sheriff's office to leave word where he'd be and, under cover of the grainy darkness, the two men pitched camp.

"No wood for a fire," Fargo said, "and it'll get cold tonight. But those boulders are hot from the day's sun, and they'll stay warm for hours. Put your back to one. Before you turn in, dig a little wallow—it'll help keep your body heat trapped under your blanket."

"You know," Sitch remarked as the two men shared a smoke, "Iron Mike Scully is going to fart blood when he sees what you did to his bootlick."

"I know that," Fargo replied. "That's why I roughed him up. Best way to cure a boil is to lance it. I don't pussyfoot once I know who my enemies are. Besides, men make stupid mistakes when they get boiling mad."

"It's the odds that make me nervous," Sitch admitted, palming the wheel of his newly acquired six-shooter. "Sheriff Vance can't be a coward—not if the Texas Rangers took him on. But he's well past his salad days and mostly seems concerned about his digestion."

"He won't likely be much use," Fargo agreed. "He's counting out the days until he gets his pension. But I was smart to talk him into deputizing me—he knows who I'm after, and

46

he knows Scully and his bunch are criminal trash. I think Vance is mostly honest, and so long as we don't get too obvious with our tactics, we'll have his blessing to put the kibosh on those red sashes."

Fargo hesitated for a few minutes before adding, "But there's some questions I want answered first. And a woman I hope we can find."

Sitch popped the cylinder of the Remington out and shook the loads into his hand. Then Fargo heard the metallic click of the hammer striking over and over on empty chambers.

"Knock that shit off," he snapped. "You never dry-fire a weapon like that. It can damage the firing pin."

"I didn't know that."

"Doesn't seem to be much you know when it comes to anything useful, except that you're some pumpkins with that whip. I'll give you that. Have you ever fired a handgun?"

"Yeah, I won an old hogleg pistol in a card game back in Arkansas. I use to plink at targets, and I did all right under twenty yards or so from the target."

"Most shootouts with a short gun are close range, so that's not too bad."

The men finished their smoke in silence, Fargo enjoying the warmth radiating from the boulder he had selected.

"Fargo," Sitch spoke up, "do you feel safe enough now for another joke?"

"All right, but if it isn't funny I'll shoot you."

"This freighter gets to a town and goes on one helluva bender, see. He gets blind drunk, and the next thing he knows he's waking up on the ground outside of a saloon, all busted up, teeth missing, nose broke, his head throbbing like an Indian war drum. The first thing he sees when he opens his eyes is these tiny little turds dancing in a circle around him.

"'Hello, there!' one of the turds sings out. 'We're living shit, and some buffalo hunter just kicked us out of you.'"

Fargo laughed appreciatively. "That's not too bad," he admitted. "I'm glad I won't have to waste a bullet on you."

Sitch stood up and walked out past the boulders to urinate. Fargo felt his eyelids growing heavy. Suddenly:

"Jesus Christ and various saints! Fargo, come see this!"

Fargo saw it the moment he cleared the ring of boulders:

out in the sky, in the direction of Rough and Ready, what appeared to be the ghostly phenomenon that the old hostler Peatross had mentioned earlier—an eerie swirling of colored lights: red, yellow, purple, amber. They wavered and shimmered, one changing into the other.

"The hell?" Sitch exclaimed. "You ever seen anything like that?"

"I've seen the northern lights and they look something like that. But this is a lot closer. I've seen rainbows do something like that, too, especially through mist or fog. But this is pitch-dark, and the moon sure's hell doesn't make rainbows."

"You don't think—?"

"Does your mother know you're out?" Fargo scoffed.

"You needn't sound so cocksure. There's plenty of things that can't be explained."

"Sure there are. I've seen streams in the Black Hills that flow uphill. I've seen sand in New Mexico that glows green in the dark. Does that mean spooks are causing it?"

A minute later the lights disappeared.

"Out near the mining camp," Fargo mused aloud. "And that blood-drained corpse Peatross carried on about—also found near Rough and Ready."

"All right," Sitch conceded. "But how could the red sashes be doing all this?"

"That's a poser," Fargo allowed. "But the real question is *why* they'd be doing all this."

The next day, the second after the vigilantes had taken Fargo prisoner, he played his deputy role to the hilt. The two men stalled their horses at the livery and Fargo patrolled the town on foot, letting the populace see their new badge toter. Sheriff Vance was right—Carson City was no outlaw hellhole, and the only incident requiring Fargo's intervention was a brawl that erupted in the middle of Main Street. He defused it with amiable humor and a minimum of violence, desirous of maintaining good relations with the denizens of Carson City.

In reality, Fargo was searching everywhere he could for that copper-haired beauty. If she had taken refuge in Carson City, she'd have to support herself somehow. He poked his head into milliner's shops, cafés, clothing stores, anyplace that might hire a woman in a boomtown.

"At least I haven't noticed any red sashes following us," Sitch remarked.

"Scully is no fool," Fargo retorted. "After what happened yesterday, the next man he sends to watch us won't be wearing his sash. Just watch for the same face showing up too often."

The two men made their first visit to the town's most bustling saloon, the Sawdust Corner. The place seemed opulent compared to most frontier watering holes. The long, S-shaped bar was of polished mahogany with a sparkling brass rail. One half of the saloon was occupied by green baize poker tables, billiard tables in good repair, and the crooked faro rig Sheriff Vance had mentioned. The other half was a large, sawdust-covered dance floor. A fancy, brass-inlaid piano was tucked into one corner with a neatly turned out man in a bowler hat pounding the ivories with evident skill.

"Look at those dime-a-dance gals," Sitch marveled as the two men paused just inside the batwings to get the lay of the place. "Most of them look like pretty schoolteachers."

The unequivocally overweight and ugly barkeep, however, was another story. He had a fat and folding face, and his linen pullover shirt outlined chest muscles that had turned into drooping tits.

"If Moses could have seen *that* face," Sitch jibed, "there'd be an eleventh commandment."

"He has to be the owner," Fargo speculated. "Nobody would hire a bar dog that scares off business. He looks like a friendly cuss, though."

"What's yours?" he enquired when both men bellied up to the bar.

"How much is a jolt of whiskey?" Sitch asked.

"Six bits."

"Six . . . Christ, that's highway robbery!"

"I don't serve panther piss here, gents, just top grade. We— Say, long-tall, is that a star on your chest?"

"I'm your new deputy, at least for a spell," Fargo replied. "How much is beer?"

"Twenty cents, but it's a big mug."

"We'll take two," Fargo decided, fishing into his pocket. "I prefer beer anyway—cuts the dust better. And give one a nappy head, wouldja?"

"Never mind the legem pone," the bartender said. "First one's on the house since you're our new lawman."

He poured out a shot of whiskey for Sitch, a moderately cold beer with a big head for Fargo.

"Name's Bob Skinner," the drink slinger added. "Welcome to Carson City, boys."

"I'm Skye Fargo. This sad case with me is Mitt McDougall, but he prefers to be called Sitch."

"Skye Fargo, huh? Yeah, I heard you were in town, but I didn't figure you for a badge."

Fargo was carefully studying the dime-a-dance gals, looking for his mystery woman. He didn't spot her, but Sitch was right—these gals put most saloon dancers in the shade. One, especially, stood out from the others: a curvaceous blonde with hair golden as new oats cascading down her back.

"You wouldn't kick *her* outta bed for eating crackers, huh?" Skinner remarked, watching Fargo stare at her. "Her name's Belle Star. She also sings like an angel. Southern gal with a nice accent. I just hired her on yesterday."

"Yesterday," Fargo repeated. "Interesting."

He studied the woman thoughtfully for a few moments, but other than being mighty easy on the eyes, this blonde bore little resemblance to the copper-haired woman he had spotted two days earlier. Then again, he had caught only a fleeting glimpse of her. Fargo couldn't recall if the fleeing woman had a Southern accent—the tension and fear in her voice were all he could remember clearly.

Sitch seized the opportunity to tell another joke. "Say, Bob, speaking of Southern women—do you know the difference between a Northern gal and a Southern gal?"

"I certainly do. A Northern gal says, 'You can have it,' but a Southern gal says 'You *all* can have it.'"

"Don't you know any better," Fargo roweled Sitch, "than to tell jokes to a bar dog? They've heard them all a million times."

Bob Skinner was indeed friendly and seemed disposed to hang around a bit for more conversation.

"I'm new in these parts," Fargo said. "Last night me and Sitch saw something mighty peculiar—these pretty-colored lights floating around in the sky out toward Rough and Ready. You ever seen them?"

Skinner polished the bar with a rag. "I sure have, just once. Others talk about them all the time, especially the miners out at the camp. I hear more and more of them are leaving because of the queer things that been happening around there. There's plenty right here in town, too, who believe Carson Valley is haunted."

"How do you size it up?" Fargo asked.

"Me? I say it's a bunch of hooey, just like them grifters who claim to read crystal balls and palms, or them bumpologists who charge two dollars to feel your skull and then swear you're going to get rich. If you got all the fools in town on your side, that's a big enough majority anywhere, brother."

Again Fargo was studying the stunning blonde. Skinner grinned. "Say, why just stare? The first dance is on me, too."

He fished around under the bar and handed Fargo several dance tickets. "Go grind against her, Deputy Fargo. I notice how most of my gals have been looking at you. I'd say Belle's just the right type for a handsome dog like you."

Fargo thanked him and strolled across the saloon. As soon as the music paused between dances, he approached Belle.

"May I have the next one?" he asked, presenting his ticket.

"I'd rather not," she dismissed him.

Fargo took in those cornflower blue eyes and had to admit they went perfectly with the blond hair. And yet, something about her creamy-lotion skin and delicately sculpted face seemed mighty familiar. But the woman he had spotted near the massacre scene had worn a blood-splotched muslin dress— a far cry from Belle's emerald green, cut-velvet dress, which made it hard to compare impressions.

"I've had a bath recently," he coaxed her. "Just one dance?"

"I'm under no obligation to dance with anyone I'd prefer not to."

"Something's a mite queer here," Fargo opined. "You're plenty cordial with the rest of these jaspers—they get smiles as big as Texas and even kisses on the cheek. But you act like I'm a smallpox blanket."

"I don't like men who are full of themselves," she dismissed him with icy hauteur.

"One of us is full of something," he agreed.

She spun away from him to accept a ticket from another man.

"Say, deputy," said a woman at Fargo's elbow. "Is she the only girl you care to dance with? You'll find me much friendlier."

Fargo turned to take in a petite brunette wearing a dark calico skirt and a crisp white shirtwaist. She was pretty with startling eyes like two black agates and lashes that curved sweetly when she fluttered them at him. Her bodice was enticingly swollen.

"It would be my pleasure, miss," Fargo assured her, taking her into his arms as the piano player struck up a lively version of "Camptown Races."

"She's a snotty bitch," the brunette informed Fargo as they twirled. "My name is Libby Snyder, by the way. And I already know that you're the tall drink of water named Skye Fargo."

"Pleased to make your acquaintance." Fargo wanted to ask Libby some more questions about the haughty Belle Star. But he was too experienced with women to show much interest—especially when Libby was purposely pressing into him ever more tightly.

"You're not like most of the yahoos who come in here," she told him. "My lands! Your muscles are hard as sacked salt. And that's not all that's hard—have you got a railroad tie in your pocket?"

"Whatever you feel down there," Fargo riposted, "is your fault. Not that I'm complaining."

"So you do like me?"

In truth, Fargo was horny enough to like just about any female with a few teeth left. This gal had all of hers and plenty of other assets as well.

"What's not to like? You're pretty as four aces and you've got too many curves to brake for. A nice smile, too."

"I hope this is going somewhere besides a dance, Deputy."

The piano player finished his tune with a fast glissando of

notes, and Fargo watched Belle Star step up onto a low stage near the piano.

"She sings, too," Libby volunteered. "And I hate to admit it, but she does a fine job of it. Stick with me for this next dance, won't you? I'm just getting . . . warmed up."

The piano player struck up "What Was Your Name in the States," and Belle Star's silvery, melodic voice made it the best rendition he'd ever heard.

"Have you got your own place?" Libby murmured.

"Unfortunately, no. How 'bout you?"

"Well, I have a room at Ma Kunkle's boardinghouse, but I share it with two other girls. Seems like I'm never alone there. But there is a place we could meet. Have you seen the old Hartley place—that house just outside of town that was lightning struck and is half burned down?"

"I noticed it today."

"Well, there's one room at the back that hasn't been damaged. There's a corn-shuck mattress in it. Some of the girls sort of, you know, use it now and then. There's a back door, too, so a person can get in without being seen. I could bring a blanket to cover the mattress so it won't be so rough."

"You just name the day and time, pretty lady, and I'll be there."

"My shift ends at eight tonight. I don't think I can wait another day."

This was a hot little firecracker, just the kind Fargo liked. "I'll be there," he promised. "Now quit pressing into me so tight, or I'm going to be embarrassed when I cross back to the bar."

Libby gave him a teasing laugh. "One thing for sure—if it's as big as it feels, there's no way you're going to hide it."

Belle's song ended to thunderous applause and cheers. As Fargo started back across the sawdust-covered floor, he sent a cross-shoulder glance toward the stage. Belle Star was watching him and quickly averted her gaze when he met her eyes.

Interesting, Fargo thought. Mighty damn interesting.

8

"That pretty little brunette," Sitch remarked as the two men emerged from the Sawdust Corner onto the bustling boardwalk, "looked like she was climbing all over you."

"We hit it off pretty good," Fargo said absently, his crimped eyes carefully surveying the town. "Take a gander across the street at the fellow plastering up a broadsheet on the front of the dance hall. He look familiar to you?"

"He does at that," Sitch replied. "Wasn't he one of the faces we saw a couple nights ago when the sashes had us prisoners?"

"That's all I needed to hear," Fargo replied, strolling purposefully across the wide thoroughfare, dodging a big freight wagon.

But the man was apparently being more vigilant than Fargo realized. He was only halfway across the street when the stranger suddenly jerked back his handgun and opened fire at the Trailsman.

Fargo bent low and lunged to one side, shucking out his Colt. But as the would-be murderer escaped, Fargo cursed his luck—the opposite boardwalk, too, was bustling and crowded, and he couldn't risk a return shot.

The man ducked down a side street, Fargo doggedly pursuing at a full run. The moment he turned the corner, another shot snapped past his ear. This street was nearly empty of citizens and Fargo returned fire. For the next ten or fifteen seconds a running gun battle ensued until Fargo's last bullet sent the man crashing face-first to the ground. When Fargo caught up to him, the thug's toes were scratching the dirt in death agony. He was already dead when Fargo turned him around for a closer look.

"Damn it to hell," Fargo muttered. He had been aiming to wound. But his slug had caught the man just left of his spine, tearing through the heart. There went any chance to beat some truth out of him.

By long habit Fargo thumbed reloads into the wheel of his six-gun before he did anything else. Then he leathered his shooter, tugged the body out of the street, and returned to look at the broadsheet, where a crowd had already gathered around Sitch. Sheriff Cyrus Vance, too, was reading the sheet.

"We're in a world of shit now," Sitch muttered to Fargo. "Those jackals out at Rough and Ready worked mighty quick. They must've paid off the newspaper."

The broadsheet was a summary of headlines from that day's *Territorial Enterprise*, published in nearby Virginia City and the most widely circulated newspaper in the Nevada Territory. Fargo read the glaring, large-print headline:

SKYE FARGO RED-HANDED MURDERER???

The story ballyhooed the massacre of the Hightower family in the typical sensational writing of that era's newspapers, substituting "eyewitness" accounts for any verified facts without identifying those witnesses. The story did not outright accuse Fargo and "his nefarious companion" of murder. But it did note that the two men were stripping the corpses when "heroic champions of law and order captured them after a bloody frolic during which hundreds of rounds were expended."

And in a touch sure to enflame frontier passions, it was broadly hinted that Sarah Hightower was "brutally outraged before being murdered," outraged being the preferred substitute for the word "raped."

"You folks clear the hell out of here," Sheriff Vance snapped at the crowd. "This is all hogwash— G'wan, clear out."

He looked at Fargo. "Let me see your toothpick."

Fargo handed him his knife and the sheriff made short work of scraping the broadsheet off.

"Go check around and make sure there's no more," Vance told Sitch. "Fargo, c'mon over to my office."

Fargo felt hostile stares following him.

"Should I send for the undertaker?" Vance asked as the two men retreated.

"Why waste the money?" Fargo replied. "I'd just feed him to the hogs."

"That would be my preference, too, but city ordinance don't allow it."

Back in the office, the sheriff dropped into the chair behind his desk and let out a long, fluming sigh. "This is bad, Fargo. We can take the broadsheets down, but now word is out all over the territory that you're a woman and child killer—and a damn rapist. Too many of these rubes believe anything that's printed in black and white."

Fargo had already figured out that much. "Yeah. They accused me of everything except roasting and eating the corpses."

"That might be coming. Those poncy men in the newspaper racket will milk this for every drop. Somehow you're going to have to clear your name before these yahoos get liquored up and fit you with a necktie."

"They've got this new Associated Press for sharing telegraphic dispatches," Fargo said. "This could spread all over the country. I've got to find that woman who escaped the attack—she's my only witness."

"Had any luck on that score?"

Fargo shook his head. "You heard of a woman named Belle Star? She was just hired on as a singer and dancer at the Sawdust Corner."

"With my pesticatin' gut, I don't spend much time in the saloons—they don't serve milk. First I've heard of her though. What, you think she might be the woman you're looking for?"

Fargo folded into a ladder-back chair, shaking his head. "Nope. The only thing I got to go on is that she was just hired. Other than the fact that she's a beauty, there's not even any resemblance. The woman I saw had copper-colored hair, this gal's a light blonde. Besides, I only got a brief squint of the woman who was running away."

"Women are scarce as hen's teeth out west," Vance pointed

out, "but not in boomtowns like Carson City. They come and go all the time looking for rich husbands."

"What I still can't figure," said a frustrated Fargo, "is why this vigilante bunch has so damn much interest in me. Sure, I gave them the slip, and likely that pissed them off. But they don't care two jackstraws about avenging that family, and besides, I don't think they really believe I killed those folks. Matter fact, I think they did it."

"That's not too low for Iron Mike Scully," the sheriff agreed. "But why would they kill the goose that lays the golden egg? Hell, they sent for Clement Hightower so he could find that supposed vein of silver for them."

"Does *any* damn thing about this deal make sense?"

The door opened and Sitch came in.

"Find any more?" Vance asked him.

"One. It was plastered up in front of the Three Sisters Saloon. There was already a crowd around it. I scraped it off with my clasp knife. There was this hombre the size of a farmer's bull that tried to stop me."

Vance cast a skeptical eye at McDougall's light frame. "And you were able to stop him?"

Sitch touched the fancy handle of the whip in his belt. "I didn't exactly stop him. I put on a little show, and the whole damn crowd was so entertained, they forgot they were mad. In fact—"

Sitch pulled a handful of coins from his pocket. "One of them passed the hat when I was done and I made almost three dollars."

The sheriff looked askance at Fargo. "He's stretching the blanket, right?"

Fargo shook his head. "He's a trick-whip expert. I've seen him in action. Sheriff, if you tied a quill on the end of that lash, he could write a book just by snapping that whip."

"Be damned. Well, whip tricks won't pull your bacon out of the fire, boys. The word's out now, and this deal is gonna get nasty."

"Yeah," Fargo agreed. "Right now, Sitch, we're down to bedrock and showing damn little color. And if we don't strike a lode mighty quick, we're gonna be getting our mail delivered by moles."

Fargo spent the remainder of that day endlessly trying to locate the mysterious copper-haired woman or at least to pry information about her out of anyone who would talk to him. But now that word of the broadsheets had swept through town like a comber, many of the residents of Carson City were openly hostile to him—a hostility that Fargo feared would soon bubble over into a lynching or at least attempts on his life.

With danger now pressing in from all sides, Fargo did not pick a new campsite until after dark, this time on the opposite side of town in a little draw ringed by juniper trees. The two men retrieved their horses from the feed stable and put them on long tethers to graze the nutritious autumn grass.

"You know, Fargo," Sitch remarked, "I don't mind sleeping on the ground and taking the risk of rattlesnakes. But this town is getting bad for our health. They say discretion is the better part of valor—why don't we just vamoose while we're still above the ground?"

"It might soon come down to the nut-cuttin'," Fargo conceded. "But like I already told you—we have to locate that damn woman. Sure, we can hightail it, and maybe this deal will just blow over. There's not one shred of legal evidence against us. Then again, that newspaper claptrap could swell up so big that we'll spend the rest of our born days south of the border wearing them foolish disguises of yours."

"I believe you're worried about clearing yourself, all right. No honest man wants a stain on his name. But I also think the massacre of the Hightower family, and what Scully and his rabid curs did to you, has got under your skin and is making you stubborn."

"What if it is?" Fargo demanded. "You helped bury those folks. And you were sentenced to drag-hang right alongside me. It doesn't stick in your craw, too?"

"I s'pose it does—killing the family, I mean. Hell, when I think of those two innocent little girls . . . those images will be painted on my eyeballs for life. And I confess I'm curious to know what's behind all this. As far as the other—I already got plenty of stains on my name, and I've escaped a lynching or two. All I feel afterward is relief, not a thirst for revenge."

"Of course not because you were guilty every time. But like I told you, you're free to cut your picket pin anytime you've a mind to. Me, I'm sticking. Anybody drunk or stupid enough to try freeing me from my soul will soon be playing checkers with Satan."

"Well, you're in the right. I just— *Katy Christ!*"

Sitch was abruptly interrupted by a hair-raising shriek that froze Fargo for a few seconds, his pulse suddenly exploding in his ears. Fargo had heard about banshees, and this long, attenuated cry sounded exactly like the unearthly sound he imagined they might make. It sounded again, and Fargo was forced to walk out and calm the horses.

"Was that an animal?" Sitch demanded when it was silent again and he found his voice.

"Not a four-legged one," Fargo replied grimly. "A Puma sends out a fearsome cry, but this one had too much warble in it. It came from the direction of Rough and Ready. More of this 'haunted valley' horseshit."

"Now see, that's one of the things I'm curious about. Who's trying to drive those miners off, and why?"

"You might's well ask me what causes the wind because I sure's hell can't tell you. If I had to guess, I'd say it's Scully and his lickspittles, but I'm damned if I can figure the why of it. I do know this—we're gonna have to start riding out to that area after dark and try to figure out what they're up to."

"Hookey Walker! Fargo, we just barely got out of that place alive!"

Fargo grinned in the generous moonwash. "Yeah. That'll give it a little more savor, huh? But no need to piss yourself— it's best if I do the nighttime spying alone. Even in broad daylight I doubt if you could locate your own reflection in a hall of mirrors."

"I'm getting smarter just watching you. But I'm damned if I'm riding back to that camp."

Fargo removed a comb from a saddle pocket and began combing his hair and beard. He had an appointment in just a few minutes with a mighty shapely brunette, and he could still feel her curves pressing into him—that familiar feminine pressure that said *I want*. Sitch had used part of his whip-trick earnings that day to purchase a bag of licorice drops and now he began chewing one.

"Here's a good one for you, Fargo. This fancy society woman goes into a Chinese laundry and demands, 'I want these clothes washed and lickety-split.' The Chinese laundryman replies, 'I washee the clothes, lady, but I no lickee the split.'"

Fargo groaned. "That one's so old, it's got dinosaur shit on it. Look, I'm heading into town for a bit. Keep your eyes and ears open, and pay close attention to my stallion. He's a good sentry. If he gets agitated, shuck out that Remington and lay low. I'll give you the hail when I return so you don't shoot me full of holes."

"I *knew* you were fussing with your hair for some good reason. You're gonna play slap 'n tickle with that brunette, are'n'cha?"

"So what? I happen to know you went upstairs at the Sawdust Corner this afternoon and got your bell rope pulled. Ain't my fault you're so damn homely you have to pay for it."

"Yeah, but say, she was worth it."

"Don't tell me," Fargo said sarcastically. "She said you were the best she ever had, right?"

"Nah. She didn't even pretend to come like most of them do. But she did laugh at my jokes—laughed real hard."

"Fine. Give me eight bits and I'll laugh at 'em too."

Fargo shucked out his Colt and palmed the wheel. Then he set off on foot in the moonlit darkness.

"You know," Sitch called out behind him, "they say it's easiest to kill a man when he's in the rut or taking a crap."

"You have definitely learned a few things," Fargo called back.

"Yeah, but have you thought about something else? I know that women flock to you like flies to syrup. But it sure seems to me that little brunette didn't waste any time getting you all het up. You told me men make stupid mistakes when they get too angry—what about men who get too horny? And what if Iron Mike has got her on his payroll to lure you into a trap?"

Fargo suddenly halted. It wasn't unusual, in his experience, for willing, wanting women to make themselves available quickly. But Libby *had* pounced mighty fast—and it was she who named the meeting place. All of a sudden it seemed like Sitch McDougall was the experienced hand and Fargo the greenhorn.

"Thank you all to hell and back," he replied sarcastically. "You *do* know how to kill a mood."

"Sorry if I spoiled your big time. But you'd better hope it's just a mood that gets killed."

9

Fargo had seen crossroads towns on the frontier that went virtually dormant after sundown. Carson City, however, like all boomtowns, was in full swing. There was the usual unbroken, raucous laughter and shouting from the saloons, the frenetic tinkling of piano notes and the tinny blast of hurdy-gurdy machines, the occasional celebratory shot. Fargo had learned that one or two shots in a boomtown were almost always innocuous, while rapid strings of three or more often meant it was time to send for the undertaker.

He avoided the town proper, swinging wide of its eastern edge and then doubling back behind the lightning-damaged house Libby had mentioned. The windows had been boarded up on the undamaged portion at the rear, perhaps by a former squatter.

Or perhaps, a nettlesome voice in his mind suggested, *by killers who don't want you to see who is inside?*

Mindful of Sitch's sinister suggestion, Fargo crouched in the silver moonlight to watch and listen. Now and then the wind gusted to a hollow moaning, but if anyone was lurking outside to kill him, his experienced senses could not detect him.

Fargo moved up to one side of a rickety back door and tapped on it, dropping his right palm to the butt of his Colt. It occurred to him that the most efficient way to murder him would be to burn him down when the door was opened.

"Is that you, Skye?" a soft, feminine voice called out.

"Yeah, it's me, Libby."

"The door's unlocked."

Fargo remained on one side and thrust it open with his foot, half expecting a hail of lead. Instead, he saw only the soft light of a single candle throwing flickering shadows onto peeling rose-pattern wallpaper. Libby sat on the cornshuck mattress she had mentioned, which was covered with a clean gray blanket.

"Why so cautious?" she teased him. "Afraid I'll bite?"

"Oh, I don't mind a little biting," he replied suggestively. "But somebody's been trying damn hard to pop me over, and I want to make sure we enjoy ourselves in peace."

"There's nobody here but us, silly."

"I trust you, cupcake, but I always cut the cards anyway."

He poked his head out of an interior door that led to a hallway. But the rest of the place had burned out and caved in on itself, leaving no place for an assassin to hide.

Fargo could almost hear Sitch's voice in his ear suggesting that maybe Libby herself was paid to kill him. But Fargo decided to roll the dice on that one—he could hardly insult the woman with his suspicions and expect to enjoy her favors.

The hallway door had a bolt lock, and Fargo slid it home. An old deal table sat alongside one wall of the undamaged room. Fargo dragged it over in front of the rear door. With the windows boarded up he now felt relatively assured that he'd have time to fill his hand with something besides tits if trouble broke out.

"You're late," she pouted as he laid his Henry near the mattress and began to unbuckle his gun belt. "I was afraid maybe you were with Belle Star."

"What, the Ice Queen? Tell you the truth, I'm surprised you showed up. By now you must've heard about that broadsheet."

"Oh, pouf! That story is a crock. None of the gals in the saloon believe it for one minute."

"Maybe, but some of the men do, right?"

Libby's skirt button-looped up the side. She began unlooping it.

"Most men are assholes, pardon my French. Bob Skinner doesn't believe it, and neither does Henry—the piano player. But a few of the usual blowhards are trying to stir up some of the other men."

At the moment the topic clearly didn't interest her. "I

63

wanted to be ready," she explained, "so I didn't wear any underclothing. It takes too long to get out of."

The skirt fell open and she spread her slender, shapely thighs wide to give Fargo the full vista. "You like?"

The flattering candlelight showed Fargo a silky triangle of mons hair crowning a love nest that already glowed with her desire.

"Damn straight I like it," he replied in a voice made husky by sudden lust. "As you can see, I'm ready, too."

He dropped his trousers and set free a straining erection that was swollen rock hard. It piston-bobbed up and down with each heartbeat that sent hot blood surging into it.

"Sakes and saints!" she exclaimed. "I knew it felt big when we was dancing, but I didn't know a man could be hung with something that large."

Fingers trembling with desire, she quickly opened her shirtwaist so Fargo could admire two beautifully sculpted, plum-tipped breasts. He dropped onto his knees beside her and pushed her down onto the mattress, burying his face in this luscious pulchritude. Head swinging like a pendulum, Fargo moved back and forth between each nipple, sucking them until they felt hard as rock candy in his mouth.

"Nibble them a little," she begged, twining her fingers into his hair to push him harder against her. "Little fish nibbles—and it's just fine if they hurt a little bit."

While Fargo played taste-tester with those firm and fine tits, Libby extended one hand and wrapped it around his man gland, stroking its curved length.

"My lands, it feels like iron! Skye, would it offend you if I get on top instead of you?"

"I don't mind working under a woman," Fargo quipped, stretching out onto his back on the mattress.

She was so fired up by now that she was panting. "Oh, but that's just the point—*I* want to do all the work. I want you to lay just as still as if you were dead. I know it sounds . . . perverse, but I get more shivers when I'm in full control."

Fargo liked this better and better. "Perverse" had never bothered him one whit.

Libby straddled him, gripping his manhood and adjusting it perfectly before she nudged the swollen purple tip past the chamois-soft portal of her cunny, both of them gasping at the explosion of galvanic pleasure.

Instead of plunging down greedily, she teased both of them by rapidly working just his glans, stimulating her swollen pearl. Her first climax was almost instant, and Fargo did indeed feel her shiver. Unable to hold this discipline she suddenly twitched her hips and took all of him to the hilt, their pubic hairs grinding together.

She bent forward far enough for Fargo to again lick, suck, kiss and nibble her tits while she rode him wilder and harder, unable to suppress her cries of ecstasy. Fargo barely twitched a muscle and didn't need to—this enflamed fox, now climaxing every few seconds, worked him with her love muscles, gripping and relaxing until the Trailsman felt that familiar, indescribable tightening and tingling between his asshole and balls that signaled imminent volcanic release.

Only now did his pleasure-overloaded body force him to move, bucking repeatedly like a mustang trying to shake the saddle off as he spent himself. Afterward, Fargo had no idea how long the two of them lay there, his mind shutting down completely in postcoital daze. Libby's tired but happy voice broke the silence first.

"Skye Fargo, I swear—if every man was as good as you, I'd become a whore tomorrow so I could have it all night long."

"Good? Me? You did everything—I just laid there."

"It was that fine cod inside me that inspired me. I hope you weren't thinking about Belle Star while I was working it?"

"Honey, I wasn't *thinking* at all. But since you brought up the subject of Belle Star . . ."

Fargo was getting desperate and he had decided to take Libby into his confidence. He told her everything about what happened at the massacre site, including his brief sighting of a beautiful woman escaping the scene.

"That woman is the only witness to what happened," he concluded. "If I can't find her, and soon, I just might be looking up to see daisies."

"But you said the hair color is all wrong."

"Yeah, but you would know this—could a woman change

her hair color so good that it would look as natural as hers does?"

"Well . . . yes. There's a few shops in town that sell very good hair dyes—some of the dance gals have done that, and you can't tell it."

"How 'bout a wig?"

"A wig might fool a man, but a woman could tell it. She's not wearing a wig."

"And those blue eyes," Fargo mused. "They do go perfect with the hair."

"'Case you haven't noticed, you big galoot, your eyes are a fetching blue, too, and you're sure no blond."

"There's a point," Fargo conceded.

"You know, Skye, there's always been talk around Carson City about this Clement Hightower fellow, and folks say he's been living up in Washington Territory. Belle Star definitely has a Southern drawl in her speech."

"Libby, very few of the folks now in the West, besides the tribes, were born here. And a good number of them hail from the South. That means nothing."

"That's true enough. I was born in Illinois, and I don't know of one gal at the Sawdust Corner who was born west of the Missouri River."

"But where could she be staying?" Fargo wondered. "Ma Kunkle's boardinghouse?"

"Could be. That's a big place, and Ma's got it divided up into at least twenty rooms. I haven't seen her there, though. It's no use in asking Ma. Most of her boarders are women, and she's very protective—she won't tell you a thing, even with you being a deputy. Somehow I don't think she's staying there—one of the other gals would have mentioned it. And her being the prima ballerina and all, she won't talk to any of the women at the Sawdust Corner."

"I s'pose there's other places to stay in town, huh?"

"Quite a few folks have rooms to let. If Bob Skinner knows, he won't let on. He's crazy in love with her, and she's got him wrapped around her little finger. A man as ugly as him is putty in the hands of a beautiful woman."

"Yeah, Bob Skinner," Fargo said. "So he's loopy on the girl, huh? That's interesting."

"You sure you're not asking all these questions because you want to get under her petticoats?"

"Libby, you know the deal. There's no red-blooded man alive that can look at any pretty girl—you included—and not immediately think about what's under her petticoats."

"That's true," she conceded. "Didn't take me long to wonder what was under your buckskins, and if women do that, men surely do."

"Believe me, that's not my main interest in Belle Star. I'm still not convinced she's the same woman I saw running away, and I might just be barking at a knot. But I would truly appreciate anything you can find out about her. Remember, if it is the same woman, she's scared spitless. She knows she's the only witness to what really happened, and the scum that killed her family won't hesitate to put the quietus on a witness."

"If it is her, Skye," Libby said, "that would explain her snotty behavior and why she stays so private, the poor thing."

"Damn straight it would. Matter fact, she's in more danger than I am. And Iron Mike Scully made a big deal out of asking me about a woman. That means him and his bunch of cutthroats are looking for her, too. If I don't find and identify her before they do, she's going to die hard. And Skye Fargo might not be far behind."

At the same time that Fargo was disporting himself with Libby Snyder in Carson City, Iron Mike Scully was sharing a bottle of forty-rod at Rough and Ready with his chief lieutenants, Romer Stanton and Leroy Jackman.

"I shoulda listened to you boys on day one," Iron Mike said. "You both told me that Skye Fargo was death to the devil. First he busts out of here a-smokin' and scatters our mounts to hell and back. Then he rides into an ambush and manages to pin down three men well hidden in boulders. Yesterday he beats Russ up so bad that he still can't move from his bedroll. And then today he guns down Deadwood Dick, one of our best shots."

"On top of all that," Jackman said in his hillman's twang, "he's got hisself made a deputy goddamn sheriff."

"I still say we just leave the son of a bitch alone," Romer put in. "He ain't got the map, so screw him."

Iron Mike Scully spat into the fire, loosing a string of creative curses. "'Course he ain't got the map, you thundering asshole! We searched him and that sad sack of shit with him, di'n't we? We went through their saddlebags, too. Unless one of them shoved it up his bunghole, they didn't have it. The problem with Fargo ain't that he's got the map."

Iron Mike took down at least two inches of whiskey and passed the bottle to Leroy.

"The problem, Romer, you ferret-faced idiot, is Fargo himself. Why do you think he pinned on that star? You think a newspaper hero like him is going to let the murder of Hightower and his family stand? Or that he's just going to sit on his prat after we tried to hang him? He means to shoot us or hang us, and you can take that to the bank."

"You think he seen the woman?" Leroy asked.

"Now there I'm neither up the well nor down. By the time he rode in, she had plenty of time to vamoose. I wish we knew what the bitch looks like. But she had to be with that family. In his letter saying he was coming down to help us, Hightower named everybody in his family that was coming with him. And he definitely mentioned a sister named Dora. It was pitch-dark when we jumped them, she could easy have slipped out taking that map with her."

"Well, she didn't go to Virginia City," Romer pointed out. "We've had two boys up there watching the only road in, and they got there way before she could've. And even a woman ain't stupid enough to flee into the desert east of us. Either she escaped toward the eastern slope of the Sierra or she's holed up in Carson City."

"I just can't see her running toward the Sierra," Iron Mike said. "That's mighty rough country and there ain't nobody living on it but grizz bears and a few trappers. What prospectors are left are way the hell up near the summit. We got no choice but to assume she went to Carson City."

"Yeah, that shines," Romer said. "But we got no proof she's got a map, or even that Clement Hightower ever made one. He said he knew where the vein is, but he never claimed to have no map."

"We got no proof your mother doesn't fuck Indians, either," Scully snapped. "But do you figure she does? Boys,

I was up on the Comstock when Clancy Munro showed me a clipping from an old newspaper, and it said Hightower did map out where that vein is. We tossed that wagon and every damn one of the bodies, and there was no map."

"There's a map," Leroy agreed. "And now Fargo knows we're looking for a woman on account we asked him about her. If he's half as smart as he seems to be, he'll track down that skirt and them two will parley. Hell, he could be in cahoots with her now."

"Sure as sun in the morning," Iron Mike agreed. "Which means he might get that map eventually. And you was stupid enough to yell out my name during the attack. If that bitch heard it, that's all Fargo will need to settle our hash. We got to find her and get that map, but unless we point Fargo's toes to the sky first, it won't be of no use to us when we're feeding worms."

The bottle made its way back around to Scully, who again took it down by a couple of inches. He wiped his mouth on the back of his hand and then loosed another string of curses.

"You know, boys, I'm starting to regret that we didn't go along with the original agreement 'steada killing that family. But that damn profit-sharing agreement he was gonna make us sign gave half the profits to him. I figured, hell, why not just get the map, scare these other stupid rubes outta the valley, and then us three could sell the whole kit and caboodle to one of them big, wha'd'ya call it, consortiums. But it looks like I opened a can of worms."

At the next campfire, voices rose in argument.

"Hear that?" Scully said. "More of them dirt pushers fighting about whether or not to pull out. At least that part of the plan is panning out. Won't be long now and there won't be enough left to keep this mining operation going. Then us three will be sitting in the catbird seat."

Romer chuckled. "This next little show I got planned will cap the climax. Half of 'em that's left are so scairt now they won't go into the woods alone after dark to take a shit."

"You're doing a good job on that," Scully allowed. "But Skye Fargo ain't the type to be scared off by haints. So we best figure out how to kill that bastard, and quick."

10

Fargo and Sitch McDougall rolled out of their blankets at sunrise before Carson City came to life for the day.

"Tack that sorrel and hop your horse," Fargo ordered. "We're riding out to take a squint around."

"A squint around where?" Sitch demanded, alarm spiking his voice. "Not back to that damn mining camp?"

"Not quite *to* it, no. Those queer lights the night before, and that damned hellacious scream last night, came from the same area. I want to take a look around."

"But how could you possibly pinpoint them? Lights and sound bounce around all over the place."

"Did I use the word 'pinpoint,' chowderhead? I make mind maps of every area I spend time in," Fargo explained after warming the bit so the Ovaro would take it without rebelling. "I got a good general idea where to look. If you really want to survive on the frontier like you claim, you'd best get chummy with geography. Memorize landmarks and terrain features, and try to map out things in your head like escape routes and ambush points."

"It all makes sense, Fargo, but how does a man learn all that?"

"Not in college," Fargo assured him. "You learn quick or you die quick. And even if you learn all of it, death is always as real as a man riding beside you."

"So why do you take the risk? A clever fellow like you could get on fine back in the States."

"Maybe because I don't cotton to the idea of paying taxes on the meat I eat."

"I don't either, but I just cheat the tax man."

"Just sew up your lips and get horsed."

"All right, but what about breakfast?"

Fargo cinched the girth and inspected the latigos. "We'll eat in town when we get back."

The two men rode out bearing northwest, patches of jack pine and juniper to their left, the already glaring alkali flats on their right. Desert nights were chilly in autumn, but the day had already heated up until the brittle air seemed to radiate from a giant furnace. Even this early, heat shimmers had begun to distort their view of the desert horizon. Closer to hand, Fargo watched a yellow-gray coyote slink off through a dry wash.

"Shouldn't we ride in the tree cover?" Sitch inquired at one point.

"That's usually the best idea, yeah. But right now I want to see what kind of prints I might find around here. Besides, those drunken sots at Rough and Ready roll out late with a hangover. The only thing we need to fret is red aborigines."

Ten minutes later they rode upon a large scattering of dung. Fargo reined in.

"All right, Daniel Boone," he said, "read the ground around here and tell me what you see."

"Well, plenty of horseshit. And I can see that the hoof-prints weren't made by shod horses."

"All right, but that leaves you two possibilities. It's a herd of wild mustangs or a bunch of Indians. How do you tell which?"

Sitch shook his head. "Flip a coin, I guess."

"All your coins got two heads on them," Fargo barbed. "If all this dung was in a large pile that would mean a herd of wild mustangs because they always stop as a group to relieve themselves. These riders are Indians because they keep their mounts on the move while they crap, and you can see the droppings are scattered in a line."

"Say, that's good to know." Sitch sent a nervous glance around them. "Are these fresh prints?"

"Nope. If you look close you'll see how the edges have crumbled and sand has started to blow into them. You can also tell that they were running their horses—the prints will be between seven and ten feet apart, and these are at least nine. They were in a hurry to get someplace."

"Likely to slaughter white men. I've heard the Paiutes in this territory are bloodthirsty savages."

"Yeah," Fargo shot back, "unlike the white curs who slaughtered those women and kids, huh?"

"We don't know for sure it was the red sashes who did that."

"Did I say *which* white curs? It wasn't bronze john who filled them folks full of big-caliber rounds. Besides, the only tribes I know of that will kill kids that small are the Apaches and Comanches—most Indians take little kids into the tribe and raise them as Indians."

"Sometimes I wonder if you're an Indian lover," Sitch remarked as the two men gigged their horses into motion again.

"Sure I am. I've 'loved' more Indians into their graves than you're likely to ever see. But you can lay a lot of the trouble with Paiutes at the feet of these white whiskey peddlers. That Indian burner they supply them ain't just cheap whiskey—it's usually laced with strychnine and makes a man crazy wild, not just drunk. I took a jolt of it once and started shooting at the moon."

Fargo led them into the scattered tree cover now as they edged closer to the camp. They slowed their horses to a walk, and the only sound was the dusty twang of grasshoppers and the eerie singsong of cicadas.

"We're close now to where those lights and that scream came from," he muttered to Sitch. "Hush down and keep a sharp eye out."

Fargo rode in slow circles, narrowing the circumference with each revolution. After about twenty minutes:

"Here's medicine," he announced with satisfaction, swinging down and tossing the reins forward.

They had discovered a small clearing, about thirty feet across, packed down with the prints of iron-shod horses and men wearing boots. Whiskey bottles and cigarette butts littered the area. Most curious, to Fargo, was the deep, narrow fire pit that had been dug in the center of the clearing—far deeper than needed to merely suppress the glow of flames. Fargo beat the bushes for a few minutes.

"Here's your 'otherworld' scream," he said. He pulled out

a wooden megaphone of the type sometimes used by auction-
eers and politicians giving stump speeches to large crowds.

"That definitely explains why it was so loud and traveled
so far," Sitch said. "But the man who did the screaming had
some gruesome talent."

"It was a variation of the Texas yell," Fargo said.

"The who?"

"The Texas yell. Texans came up with it for fighting Mexican soldiers, and later the Texas Rangers had a version of it
they used to unnerve Comanches and Kiowas when they
were closing in on them. I didn't place it at first, but that's
what it was."

"Still doesn't explain those strange lights," Sitch pointed
out.

"Nope. But if this scream was made by men working a
scam, the lights were too. Hold on—here's something else."

Fargo rummaged into a pile of dead leaves and pulled out
an accordion-folded bellows of the type used by blacksmiths
to stoke a fire hotter.

"The hell?" Sitch said.

Fargo mulled these discoveries for a minute, glancing at
the fire pit. "It's got something to do with that fire pit and
whatever's causing those floating lights."

"What about corpses drained white of their blood?"

"If you pierce a man's jugular," Fargo said, "without
killing him first, the heart will pump out enough blood
before he dies to make it look like he was sucked dry of
blood."

"Scully and his bunch?"

"I'd bet my horse on it," Fargo said. "But right now we
can't prove it. That doesn't bother me half as much as trying
to figure out the why of it."

Fargo hid the megaphone and bellows back where he'd
found them.

"Why are you leaving them here?" Sitch demanded.
"Shouldn't we at least destroy them?"

"Use your noodle, jughead. Look, we have to pick cotton
before we can make cloth. If we take this stuff, or wreck it,
these sage rats will move to another spot. And we want witnesses to see this stuff. First, though, I'm coming back here

after dark to spy on them while they make those lights. I got a hunch how they might be doing it."

Fargo gazed around the area for perhaps another thirty seconds, his brow wrinkled in concentration. Then he took up the reins and forked leather. He tugged rein and started down their backtrail.

"Proving who did it, and why, will have to wait for now," he told Sitch. "First we ride back to Carson City and get outside of some hot grub. And then I'm going to annoy the hell out of a very pretty lady."

The two men left their horses at Peatross's feed stable and then grabbed a quick meal of eggs and side meat. While Sitch roamed the town looking for any more incriminating broadsheets, Fargo headed toward the Sawdust Corner.

The moment he slapped open the batwings, he felt hostile eyes on him. He had covered half the distance to the dance floor when a bullnecked man at one of the poker tables called out, "Hey, Deputy? How much do you get for a dead-baby pelt?"

Snickers and guffaws rippled through the saloon. Fargo veered toward the table and stared at the speaker until the man nervously averted his eyes.

"*You* appear to be full grown, you mouthy piece of shit," Fargo said in a cool, level tone. "No need to take the long way around the barn—go ahead and call me a woman and child killer to my face. If you think that's what I am, then why mealymouth?"

"I got no dicker with you," bull neck replied.

Fargo's penetrating blue gaze had hardened to a point that no man could mistake. "Well I got one with you. Now swallow back those words or step out into the street."

"I take it back."

Fargo's gaze swept the entire saloon. "I didn't ride into this town to offend any man. But any of you good old boys who are planning to stir up the shit against me had best cogitate real careful like. You'll soon be wearing new suits—the kind with no back in them."

Libby Snyder left the dance floor and took Fargo's elbow, guiding him to one side.

"Skye, some of that red sash bunch came in here earlier.

They took off the sashes, but I recognized them. They were studying all of the dance gals, and they had a special interest in Belle Star."

"Did they talk to her?"

"No. They seemed nervous and kept watching the entrance—I think they were skittish about you coming in."

Another angle occurred to Fargo. "How 'bout the soiled doves topside? Any new arrivals?"

Libby shook her head. "There's six sporting gals, and the newest one is Jenny Tolbert. She's been here over a month. But be careful if you go up there—some stranger went up there, and he still hasn't come down yet. I can't place him as one of the sashes, but he seemed to come in with the others."

"How long ago did he go up?"

"It's been at least an hour, and very few men spend more than ten minutes if they're getting a poke."

Fargo nodded, his lips forming a grim, determined slit. "What's he look like?"

"A thin, hard-looking man with these little pig eyes set way too close together. He's mostly bald but combs what hair he's got left over his dome to hide it."

"Thanks, Libby," Fargo said.

Fargo headed toward the stairway built against a side wall of the saloon. Saloon noise covered the creaking of the lumber steps, but Fargo ascended slowly, loosening his Colt in the holster.

As he approached the dimly lit landing, Fargo felt his scalp prickling in the familiar warning his body often sent to his brain. He shucked out his six-gun and took the last few steps on full alert.

There were three doors, numbered one through six, opening onto both sides of a narrow, dim hallway that smelled of beeswax and cheap perfume. But a seventh door at the far end of the hall wasn't numbered. There were no obvious signs of danger, but something definitely felt off-kilter. With a metallic click Fargo thumb-cocked his Colt.

Slowly he started down the hall, making sure each door was solidly closed. Behind the door numbered 2 he heard the artificial cries of ecstasy as a painted lady urged a john toward release.

Halfway down the hallway, with the unnumbered door looming closer, Fargo felt his pulse thudding hard in his palms. He had faced every manner of danger on the frontier, ranging from enraged grizzlies to sudden Indian attacks. And yet, one of his greatest fears remained closed doors. On one side was the known and visible, the world a man still controlled. On the other lay a different world—a world of potential, violent death. And only a thin slab of wood divided one from the other.

Fargo, heart surf-crashing in his ears, went down onto his knees on one side of the door. He took a deep breath, grabbed the glass knob, and flung the door open.

Even fully prepared for danger, Fargo flinched violently when a deafening racket of gunfire opened up only inches above his head. He fired two shots dead center on the shadowy form inside the room. Screams erupted from the rooms behind him as a body flopped heavily onto the floor beside him.

Fargo knocked the gun a few feet away from the man's hand and tugged him over just in time to watch the would-be killer's pig eyes lose their vital focus and then glaze over like glass when he gave up the ghost. Evidently one of Fargo's bullets had struck a major artery. In the shocked silence that followed the sudden outburst of gunfire, he could hear the obscene liquid-slapping sound of blood splashing onto the floor.

"Nice try," Fargo muttered.

Fargo's visit to Belle Star was put on hold as he reported the killing in the Sawdust Corner to Sheriff Cyrus Vance.

"Fargo," Vance said wearily as he filled a glass from the pitcher of milk on his desk, "that's two men you've killed right here in town since you pinned that star on and a third you beat senseless. Me and you both know that both killings were in self-defense. But it's starting to look, to some of these hotheads in town, like maybe you're killing the witnesses to your supposed massacre of the Hightowers."

"I can't help that, Sheriff," Fargo replied. "If I let all the assholes in town direct my actions, I'd be dead. You can't make an omelet without breaking a few eggs."

"No, I reckon not. But now I got pressure from the big toffs on the City Council to send you packing. Hell, I'm drinking so much milk that I'm afraid I'll start mooing soon."

The sheriff banged open the top drawer of his desk and handed Fargo a few silver coins. "Here's some of that running-around money I promised you. You—"

The door to the office groaned open and Sitch entered, wearing a new conk cover of soft felt broad as a sombrero.

"Well, if it ain't Benito Juarez," Vance greeted him sarcastically. "When you robbed that fellow of his hat, did you boost his horse, too?"

"I won it fair and square, Sheriff," Sitch protested. "We drew for top card—he drew a queen and I drew an ace."

Sitch avoided Fargo's eyes. The Trailsman had already seen that special deck Sitch carried for drawing cards—the top card was a queen, the other fifty-one cards were aces.

"Fargo," the sheriff resumed, "I'm still backing you in this deal. And I'll buck the City Council as long as I can. But if they give me the boot, there goes my measly pension and that's all I'll have to live on. Son, for Christsakes, don't let no grass grow under your feet. If this thing drags on, they'll appoint a new sheriff and we'll both be shit out of luck."

This aging lawman might have a weak stomach, Fargo thought, but he had a strong will to see justice done. Fargo admired that a hell of a lot more than bulging muscles. The frontier needed more men of conscience like this one.

"Sheriff," Fargo assured him as he headed toward the door, "I'll work night and day to tie a ribbon on this deal. This town is starting to turn on me, and I know I've got damn little time and plenty of questions to answer. And I mean to get some of them answered right now."

11

The moment the last piano notes of "Listen to the Mockingbird" fell silent, Fargo stepped in front of Belle Star and offered a dance ticket. The blonde looked stunning in a wine-colored dress trimmed with velvet, her hair swept back and held by tortoiseshell pins.

"Sorry, Deputy Fargo." She brushed him off in that melodic, softly Southern voice like waltzing violins. "I'm due for my hourly break."

She started to swerve past him just as the piano player launched into a lively rendition of "The Blue Tail Fly."

Fargo gripped her arm and swept her back onto the dance floor. "This is one of my favorite tunes. We can't miss this one."

"Let me go, you big ape!" she protested.

Fargo ignored her, manhandling her more than dancing. "There's no reason to insult me, Belle. I s'pose Belle *is* your real name?"

"Of course not. How exotic is a saloon singer and dancer named Samantha Urbanski? Let me *go*, I told you!"

"What will you do if I don't?" he goaded her. "Call in the law? After all, I'm a peace officer."

"Yes, we all witnessed your version of 'peace' when the undertaker dragged out that body from upstairs."

"He required killing . . . Samantha. I didn't go up there to make the undertaker richer."

She had finally quit resisting him and was now gracefully dancing. But Fargo could almost whiff her anger above the delightful odor of her honeysuckle perfume. And if this was the same woman Fargo had seen escaping from the massacre site several days ago, where did all her fine clothing come from? That frightened woman had not even carried a carpetbag.

Just then Fargo glanced toward the bar and saw Bob Skinner watching the woman from the sappy face of a fool in love. Libby Snyder had already told him the hopelessly ugly barkeep was in love with the woman who called herself Belle Star. That might explain the clothing—and perhaps the woman's unknown residence.

"You're a fine dancer," Fargo told her, "and I'd rate you aces high as a singer, too."

"I shall forever treasure that compliment in the locket of my heart," she replied in a tone heavily laced with sarcasm.

"Is there some special reason why you act like you smell an outhouse when I'm around? I don't recall ever insulting or mistreating you. Or did somebody steal your rattle when you were a baby?"

"Just because loose women like Libby Snyder succumb to your supposed charms, don't expect me to," she said archly.

"I'm flattered," Fargo shot back, "that you follow my activities so closely."

"Malarkey! The shameless hussy practically copulated with you right on the dance floor. I heard the other girls tittering about how she disappeared last night and then returned to her room in a state of pure bliss. Everybody knows about that deserted house on the edge of town."

"Pure bliss, huh? Well, it's nice to have good references," Fargo said slyly. "Say, I'm just a mite curious. Why would a haughty miss like you suddenly show up in Carson City working as a saloon girl? Don't tell me you plan to catch a husband here? The men who frequent boomtown saloons aren't exactly what you'd call the opera set."

"If it's any of your business, Mr. Fargo, and it certainly isn't, I just *lost* my husband. His name was James Urbanski, and he was a lawyer. We were on our way to Sacramento so he could join some friends in a law practice there. We were attacked by Indians and he was killed. I had hidden under some quilts in the back of our wagon and somehow the Indians missed me when they ransacked it. A party of freighters rescued me and brought me to Carson City. I'm here only long enough to earn stagecoach fare to Sacramento."

Her story sounded well rehearsed, but Fargo knew it was a crock. Indians didn't miss a damn thing when they ransacked, and they would never have left quilts behind. Blankets of any kind were highly prized.

"You're telling me that you and your husband were crossing the Nevada desert by yourselves?"

"It's a free country, isn't it? We were well equipped for the journey."

"I'll tell you what," Fargo forged on. "Sacramento isn't all that far from here. I know the best routes over the sierra. I'll take you myself."

"Oh, I'm sure you would *take* me."

"Lady, you're just whistling into the wind. You aren't afraid I'll rape you, but you *are* afraid of me."

"Why don't you just quit skating around the edges, Deputy? Since when are rugged men like you so coy?"

"All right," Fargo said, "I'll give it to you with the bark still on it . . . Miss Hightower."

His use of that name struck her with the force of a slap. He felt her stiffen in his arms, saw a vein suddenly pulse in her slim white throat. But this lasted only a few seconds before she composed herself.

"My name is *not* Hightower," she assured him. "I have no idea what you are fishing for."

"I think you're trapped in one helluva dirty corner," Fargo said. "Maybe your name isn't Hightower, but you were definitely with the Hightower family when they were slaughtered."

She was a fine actress and back in full control now. The faint shadow of a smile touched her full, heart-shaped lips.

"Mr. Fargo, you have a fertile imagination. Instead of playing the hero of those cheap novels, perhaps you should be writing some."

Fargo's voice hardened. "Look, lady, whatever the hell your name is—you're not half as smart as you think you are. It's easy to snow a love-struck fool like Bob Skinner. Once you start batting those pretty blue eyes at him, he doesn't care whether you're lying or not. That idiotic story you told about crossing the Nevada desert and surviving an Indian attack wouldn't fool a government mule."

"You—"

"Shut up and listen to me. You've dyed your hair, but you're the woman I saw escaping from the massacre. I don't blame you for all the lies because you're scared out of your wits. You're afraid that if I prove your identity, those murdering jackals out at Rough and Ready will kill you to eliminate the only witness to their crime. But I've got news for you—they already have their eye on you, and they'll sure as hell be asking plenty of questions."

"This is just—"

"Whack the cork," Fargo snapped. "There's more to it than what I just said. I've turned this thing over and over, and you being afraid is not motivation enough to avoid seeking protection from the law. In fact you'd be safer if you did that. There's something else that's got you scared to reveal who you are. And I've also got a hunch that Iron Mike Scully and his bootlicks aren't searching for you just to kill you— they think you have something they want, something they didn't find after they killed the others."

This time she managed to wrench free of his arms. Her nostrils flared in indignant anger.

"You've had your ridiculous say. You are either insane or completely misapprehending the truth. Now *you* listen to me. You did a fine job, earlier today, of intimidating the men in this saloon. But if you don't leave me alone at once, I'm going to start screaming my head off. And I'm going to accuse you of threatening to rape me. I think you know what that means in a Western town, especially as there is already talk that you are a rapist."

She was right and Fargo knew it. While a soiled dove, for most men, did not fall under the code of frontier chivalry, this elegant beauty certainly did. If she carried out her threat, he would be turned into a sieve before he got ten feet away.

"I surrender," he told her. "But if you think I'm your greatest danger, you've got it hindside foremost. You're going to need help before this is over, and if you wait too long help won't matter. You're going to have to take somebody into your confidence, and nobody keeps a confidence better than me."

He tossed her a two-finger salute and turned away.

Fargo dutifully patrolled the streets of Carson City for the remainder of the day, ever mindful of Sheriff Vance's warning that time was quickly running out. That warning was also clear in the small groups of men now congregating at various points in town. There was no question whom they were talking about—all conversation halted anytime Fargo passed nearby.

Always one to take the bull by the horns, Fargo boldly approached one of these gatherings outside the Three Sisters Saloon, one of the rowdier establishments in town.

"You boys having a nice discussion?" he greeted them.

"Is there some law against men congregatin' on street corners?" demanded a straw-haired man with a North & Savage rifle clutched in his right hand.

"Didn't say there was, did I? But there is a law against inciting a lynching in a town that already has law."

"Look, *Deputy*," straw hair replied, obviously the mouthpiece for the group, "we all heard about your warning in the Sawdust Corner this morning—no need to chew your cabbage twice."

Fargo's eyes, two hard gems, bored into the troublemaker until he glanced away. "Yeah, and that warning still stands. I'm just here to ask you good citizens a question: do you believe every damn thing you read in a newspaper?"

"They can't print nothing that ain't true," another man volunteered.

"What turnip wagon did you just fall off?" Fargo demanded. "You know where those ink scribblers get their so-called 'Wild West' stories? They hang around saloons and then print the most exciting bullshit that catches their fancy. It ain't but a couple hours ride between here and Virginia City. A piece of shit from that red-sash trash was sent up there, and likely all it took was a few drinks and a twenty-dollar gold piece to get some sweet-lavender pussy to concoct that story about me."

"Those sashes are trash, all right," a third man chimed in. "But all we got is your say-so it's a lie."

"And all your talk about rope justice is based on the say-so of a liar who didn't print one damn fact to back his claims. Let's just cut down to the bone, boys—you're all bored. Ain't nothing too exciting going on, and a lynching is just the ticket. Just answer me this: If any of you were low-down enough to slaughter an innocent family a few miles from here, would you ride into Carson City? Or would you hightail it to a safer place?"

A long silence ensued. But straw hair clearly did not like to lose a pissing contest.

"Let's turn that around, Fargo. If a man did murder all those folks, what better way to throw the crime on some-body else than to come into town and pin on a star? You wouldn't be the first murdering son of a bitch to hide behind a badge."

Fargo nodded. "I can't gainsay that. But I'm going to give you about ten seconds to rethink that 'murdering son of a bitch' crack before I turn this into a call-down."

The loud mouth frowned. "It was just a way of speaking. I didn't mean you in especial."

Fargo nodded. "We're square on that point. But I'll say it again: there ain't one soft-handed peckerwood among you who really believes I wiped out that family. You're just look-ing to create a little excitement. But far better men than you have tried to douse my wick, and I've sent every damn one of them over the range. So before you brave bastards get up your mob . . ."

Fargo pulled the spare cylinder for his Colt from his pos-sibles bag. "I got twelve Kentucky pills for this short iron." He hoisted his Henry higher. "And sixteen more in this fire stick. You can do the arithmetic—that's twenty-eight men who are gonna die screaming with gutshots. So you best ask yourselves—am I willing to bet that I'll be man number twenty-nine?"

Fargo spun on his heel and walked away. Sitch had emerged from a barbershop and listened to the end of this confrontation. He fell into step beside Fargo.

"What's the scam, Fargo? Think that'll keep the war ket-tle from boiling over?" he asked.

"Nope. Might bring it to a slower boil, though. It's too easy for hotheads like straw hair to stir up these town folk. But even if they decide not to jerk me and you to Jesus, this story about us being women and child killers will dog us like an afternoon shadow. We got no choice but to prove who really pulled that massacre."

Fargo fell silent, his eyes carefully scanning for trouble while his mind conned this mess over, separating the known from the speculative. At least he was now certain that Belle Star was the elusive woman he was seeking. And almost certainly it was Scully and his red sashes who were "haunting" Carson Valley to scare off more and more miners although Fargo wasn't certain why.

More important, he was convinced by now despite the apparent illogic of it that Scully and his bunch had killed Clement Hightower and his family. But why? Hightower was the mining engineer they supposedly needed to locate that rumored big silver vein.

He had separate pieces but could not make them fall into place and provide the big picture. What secret was Belle Star hiding, a secret important enough to keep her from seeking protection? And what about Fargo's nagging hunch that the sashes wanted more from her than merely killing her to shut her up? By now they must have realized that she hadn't gone to the law, so why the intense interest in her?

"This shit's for the birds," he told Sitch in a disgusted tone before he reported on his earlier conversation with Belle Star.

Unfortunately, more bad news awaited them when they stopped at the feed stable after dark to retrieve their mounts.

"Some unsavory type was watching the paddock today," old man Peatross reported. "Seemed to have a special interest in the Ovaro and that sorrel."

"He say anything to you?" Fargo asked.

"Yep. Made a point of asking me how's come them two horses was never stalled nights. He musta snuck into the barn while I was sleeping to know that."

Fargo looked at Sitch. "That means they've figured out that we're camping outside of town at night."

"So what do we do?"

"For tonight at least we'll be safest sleeping right here in the livery with the horses. The sashes will be looking for our camp. But I'm worried about the turn this trail is taking. We can't afford to roost hereabouts any longer, Sitch."

"Yeah, that's the best way to avoid a rope, all right."

"I'm not so worried about that. Sheriff Vance is about to be cashiered because of me. I'll turn in this badge tomorrow and we'll camp farther out in the rougher country."

"But you said we needed to be in town so—"

"Oh, we'll still be riding in now and then. But a man can't conquer the world from his own front porch."

Sitch's face became a mask of confusion. "Is that what we're doing—trying to conquer the world?"

Fargo expelled a long, weary sigh. "No. But would it be any harder than this deal we're caught up in now?"

12

Fargo and Sitch passed that night without incident, sleeping in a straw-lined stall near their horses. Bright and early the next morning they visited Sheriff Vance and Fargo turned in his badge.

"Fargo," the sheriff said reluctantly, "I didn't mean to run you off with that little talk yesterday."

"I know that, Sheriff. And I won't be running off until me and the horse thief here clear our names. There's a few other things that have to be cleared up, too, and I'll try like hell not to step on your toes. But Iron Mike Scully has got plenty of irons in the fire, and every damn one of them is somehow connected."

Fargo omitted the details of his talk with Belle Star. But he filled the lawman in on the recent discovery of the megaphone, the bellows and the meeting place near Rough and Ready.

"It's the sashes who are 'haunting' this valley," he concluded, "and I got no doubt it was them who killed the Hightower family. Never mind that it doesn't seem to add up. Scully is on to something big, so big that he's packing heaven with fresh corpses, including women and kids. Yeah, you're right that I got personal scores to settle with him. But this is a lot bigger than just him trying to execute me and Sitch."

Vance took a sip of milk and cast his eyes downward.

"I know you're right, Fargo. Hell, even quicksand would spit Scully back up. I've known for some time that him and that red sash bunch are lawless schemers, and I have tried to poke into this thing. But, son, I just ain't the man I use to be. Just one hour pounding a saddle and I can barely climb off my horse. Hell, nowadays I have to fill my canteen with milk. I'm retiring at the end of this year and leaving this job to a younger man. But I'll tell you straight from the shoulder—I trust you, and you got my blessing to handle this in your own way."

The sheriff shifted his gaze to Sitch. "As for you—if you wasn't siding Fargo, I'd've jugged you by now. You're trouble on two sticks."

"He is," Fargo agreed. "And he's beyond reforming. But I got a hunch he'll come in handy before this deal is over. He's green but he's got grit in him. Once in a while he gets off a good joke, too."

Sitch brightened. "Say, speaking of jokes—here's a good one I heard in the Three Sisters. This old rancher walks into the tack room and catches his fifteen-year-old boy playing with himself. 'Son,' he says sternly, 'you'd better stop doing that right now or you'll eventually go blind.' 'Pa,' the boy replies, never missing a stroke, 'how 'bout if I quit when I need glasses?'"

The sheriff cast a baleful eye at Fargo. "Is that one of his better jokes?"

Fargo chuckled. "I thought it was pretty good."

"Every man to his own gait. Here, Fargo, take this before you go. You'll be needing it."

The sheriff banged opened the desk drawer and handed Fargo two half-eagle gold pieces. "Ten bucks won't buy you the moon, but maybe it'll help you out."

"'Preciate it," Fargo replied. "Now we can lay in some grub."

Back out on the boardwalk Sitch said, "We going to find a camp now?"

Fargo shook his head. "Not until after dark. I don't want to give those sashes any chance to locate us. We'll just stick around town and let trouble come to us."

They swung into a mercantile and Fargo purchased coffee, cornmeal, dried fruit, sacks of jerky and hardtack, salt and whiskey. As they carried the supplies back to the livery, Sitch remarked:

"K. T. Christ, look at all those men giving us the hoodoo eye. I'm glad we're getting the hell out of town soon."

Fargo sent him a sly grin. "You might not be so glad, whip boy. We're not going into hiding. We're gonna be stirring up the shit, and, mister, I mean stirring it up good."

The two men killed time that day drifting from saloon to saloon, sipping a beer at each watering hole, their presence reminding the local hotheads that tough talk was cheap. But Fargo knew that the Sawdust Corner was the real magnet for trouble, and toward sundown they ambled through the batwings.

"No tin star?" Bob Skinner greeted Fargo before plunking down a mug of beer with a nappy head.

"Kept me on too short a tether," Fargo replied. "Sometimes a man needs to open from a gallop to a run."

"I take your drift, Trailsman. I heard that little speech you gave in the bar yesterday. That jasper you ventilated upstairs—I recognized him when they hauled him out. His name was Butch Soss, a hired killer from Virginia City. He wasn't a red sash, but Mike Scully is—was—his cousin."

"Interesting," Fargo said. "But no big surprise."

Skinner's fat and folded face leaned closer across the bar, and he lowered his voice. "There's a rumor Iron Mike himself and some of his boys will be coming in tonight. I know your reputation, Fargo, but take my word for it—nobody in these parts can handle a six-gun like Scully. Watch that son of a bitch like a hawk."

"I'm a peace-loving man," Fargo said from a deadpan and Skinner grinned.

"Try not to shoot my backbar mirror," he said. "That gilt trim cost me a fortune."

"Any chance on another free whiskey?" Sitch wheedled the barkeep, staring with distaste at his beer. "I been drinking this barley pop all day, and all it does is make me piss."

"Nix on the whiskey," Fargo said. "You'll need your wits about you tonight."

Skinner waited on a few customers, then wandered back toward Fargo. The Trailsman had been waiting to bring up a certain topic, and the talk about Mike Scully gave him an opening.

"You know," he remarked casually, "Libby Snyder tells me the red sashes seem to have a special interest in Belle Star."

Skinner used a rag to wipe up some beer slops, his eyes

running from Fargo's. "Can you blame them? If she was any prettier she'd be illegal."

"Oh, she is that, all right. But Scully's interest in her runs deeper than that. I think maybe he's guessed she's not exactly who she says she is. I have too."

"That's too far north for me," Skinner said evasively. "Just who do you think she is?"

Fargo recounted the tale Belle had told him yesterday while they were dancing.

"That's what she told me too," the bartender said, letting it go at that.

"Dob, I've never met a stupid bartender. You can't possibly believe that foolish pack of lies. I think she's confided in you, at least a little, and I think you're protecting her. Don't know as I blame you, either. The gal's in trouble, big trouble, and you're scared for her. But sometimes a man with the best intentions can make things worse."

Skinner mulled all that, his face a mask of indecision.

"Yeah, I know the story she gave both of us is pure twaddle and bunkum. You're wrong about one thing though—she hasn't confided in me even though I've begged her to. But she's a damn scared woman on her own in dangerous country, and I figure she must have good reasons for lying. And I'll tell you this much, too: I believe she's a good, decent woman despite the lies."

"That gets my money, too," Fargo agreed.

"Tell you something else," Skinner said. "I've noticed she's cold as last night's mashed potatoes around you, and I find that hard to figure. She's friendly with all the other men on the dance floor though she does ignore the other girls. But until I know a little more about all this, Fargo, I don't know from nothing."

Fargo nodded. "Fair enough."

By now Fargo realized that, unless Skinner was a superb liar, the barkeep didn't know about the bloodied woman who had escaped from the massacre site days ago. He also suspected, however, that Skinner knew exactly where she was staying. But it was obvious he was hopelessly in love with the beauty, and exceedingly worried about her, and Fargo didn't have the heart to press him any longer on the subject.

"Man alive, is he smitten," Sitch remarked when the barkeep moved down the S-shaped bar to pour some drinks. "Speaking as a homely bastard myself, I'm never foolish enough to fall in love. That's why the Lord made whores."

"There's homely women, too," Fargo reminded him. "And plenty of them look mighty fine from the neck down. Fall in love with one of them."

"Now, see, that's where you handsome sons of bitches go off the rails. A homely man hankers after the same beauties you do—we ain't blind, for Christsakes."

"I've screwed plenty of homely women," Fargo assured him. "And older women, too. All I require are willing volunteers above the age of consent and below the age of indifference."

"Well, it is true that all cats look alike in the dark. You know, I once poked a beautiful gal that was born without any legs."

Fargo looked at him askance. "This is leading into another joke, right?"

"My hand to God it's not! Nothing from her hips down. She was pretty as the dickens, too. She was all het up to do it, and when I asked her the best way, she told me her arms were strong and just to let her hang from a tree branch and I could do her standing up. So that's just what I did."

Fargo waved all this off. "Good thing I'm wearing boots."

"It's the truth, I swear it. And when I took her home her father thanked me several times. When I asked him why he was so grateful, he says, 'Son, they usually leave her hanging in the tree.'"

In spite of himself, Fargo cracked a grin. The next moment, however, the levity ended when the batwings swung inward and Iron Mike Scully strolled inside, accompanied by Leroy Jackman and Romer Stanton. Jackman carried his big Hawken gun, Stanton his Sharps fifty.

Fargo turned halfway around and stood hip-cocked against the bar. All three men deliberately ignored him and Sitch, staring toward Belle Star as she wound into the finish of a fine rendition of "Oh! Susanna."

Fargo had to admit Scully was a fearsome sight with his necklace of grizzly claws and the pair of ivory-handled Navy

Colts tied down low in cutaway holsters. His eyes finally flicked toward Fargo and he flashed that cruel, thin-lipped smile that failed to include the corners of his mouth. The rest of the saloon had grown as quiet as the piano.

"Well, now," Scully called toward Fargo, "how's my favorite boy?"

"Sassy as the first man breathed on by God," Fargo replied amiably.

"Lose your badge someplace, buckskins?"

"It outgrew its usefulness," Fargo replied.

Belle Star had started to step off the stage.

"Hey, blondie!" Scully shouted. "How's 'bout another tune?"

She ignored him, crossing to a door under the stairway and disappearing.

"That bitch ain't too friendly, Bob," Scully said to the bartender. "When did you hire her on?"

"A while back," Skinner replied.

"Well, say, is she one of the upstairs gals?"

"Nope. A singer and a dancer."

Scully nudged one of his companions. "I say don't hang your best meat in the window if it ain't for sale, eh, Romer?"

Scully nodded toward the door through which Belle Star had disappeared. "What's back there?"

"Just the room where the gals change."

"Yeah? Think I'll get me a free peek."

He had taken perhaps four steps before Bob Skinner reached under the bar and produced a sawed-off double ten. "It's my responsibility to protect my girls, Mike. Touch the door and I'll blast you to wolf bait."

Scully laughed. "Shit, come down off your hind legs, porky."

Scully again stared at Fargo.

"He's aching something fierce to put sunlight through you," Skinner muttered. "But he ain't quite sure of himself yet. Watch his eyes, Fargo. That'll tell you when he's decided to pull down on you."

"You never watch a gunman's eyes, Bob. That's nickel-novel crap. You watch his hands. Eyes can't clear leather."

Scully and his minions bellied up to the bar, crowding in close to Fargo. Scully gave Sitch a quick size-up.

"Fargo, you can sure pick 'em. Is this runt wearing a *hat*? Looks to me like something a Mexer catamite would wear."

"It's foolish," Fargo agreed. "But take a gander at his nice new Remington—maybe you've seen that gun before? I believe you and the previous owner, rest his soul, were feeding at the same trough. Now he's joined your cousin, the late Butch Soss, in the everlasting."

At this goading, delivered with Fargo's smile that wasn't really a smile, Scully's piercing eyes went smoky with rage.

"Yeah. And I also hear that the gent who owned that Remington was shot in the back."

"Oh, that's a mere technicality," Fargo assured him. "See, the bullets came out the front, so there were holes on both sides. Sort of like the woman and kids that were massacred a few days back—you remember them, don't you?"

This roused Scully's indignation to such a pitch that his face bloated with rage. He tossed back his whiskey and pushed his big, heavily muscled frame back from the bar.

"Tell you what, Bob," he said to the barkeep. "If that blond bitch ain't gonna sing us another tune, *I'll* provide the entertainment. Romer, grab a poker chip off that table."

"Shit," Skinner said to Fargo. "He's done this one before." In a louder tone Skinner added: "Mike, don't shoot through the ceiling. Last time you nearly killed one of my doves."

"Don't worry about the poon, Bob. I'll shoot into the floor this time."

Fargo had guessed what was coming. The "poker chip drop" was a favorite of saloon show-offs all over the frontier. A man placed the chip on the back of his gun hand, flipped his wrist to drop it, then drew his short iron and shot it as many times as he could before the chip hit the floor. Because the single-action guns of that era had to be cocked for each round, a man was lucky to get one shot off. Fargo had once watched a fabled gunman in Santa Fe get two shots off, an impressive performance.

Smirking at Fargo, Iron Mike Scully placed the poker chip on the back of his right gun hand, flipped his wrist to drop it, and then drew in a blur of speed and fanned his hammer, shooting three bullets into the floor before the chip plinked down. The saloon erupted in cheers and whistles.

Fargo, astounded, glanced at Sitch. "If I hadn't just seen that with my own eyes, I wouldn't believe it."

"Same here. Can you match that?"

"Sure, just like an oyster can walk upstairs."

"Well, I can top it."

Sitch stepped away from the bar and slid the fancy whip from his belt. "Hey, Romer," he called out to the ferret-faced lackey, "grab five more chips off that table and flip 'em into the air."

Romer glanced at his boss. Scully, curious, nodded permission. Romer flipped the chips up, and Sitch's whip cracked with amazing rapidity. All five chips flew behind Bob Skinner and clattered onto the duckboards behind the bar.

This amazing feat capped the climax, and the bar erupted in a thundering ovation.

"Don't be shy about passing the hat, boys," Sitch said when the place had quieted down a bit.

Even the hard-bitten Iron Mike Scully was visibly impressed. "Runt, that's the damnedest thing I ever seen!"

A few moments later, however, realizing he'd just lost face, he shifted his attention to Fargo again. "So that's how it is? The great Skye Fargo hiding behind the skirts of a little gal-boy?"

Fargo calmly stepped away from the bar, flexing the fingers of his right hand. "I'm not a trick shooter, Scully—I'm a kill shooter. If you're feeling froggy, go right ahead and jump."

Scully stared into that crop-bearded face and realized that Fargo had no more fear in him than a rifle. For the first time that night self-doubt revealed itself in the vigilante's eyes.

"I'm not calling you out, Fargo—not now. But the worm will turn."

Fargo, on a sudden hunch, decided to run a bluff. It was an opportunity to test a theory and perhaps even take some of the heat off the woman who called herself Belle Star.

"It's a smart idea not to be in such a hurry to kill me, Scully. Just maybe I've got something you want real bad—something hidden so good that you'll never find it if you snuff my wick."

Gratification surged through Fargo when he saw the startled

look on Scully's face. It lasted only a few moments, but that was all the time Fargo needed to confirm a suspicion.

"You're off your chump, Fargo. You got nothing I want."

Fargo continued as if Scully had never spoken, raising his voice so the entire saloon could hear him. "And I'm not ready to kill you just yet, either. Among other things, I'm gonna prove that you and those no-dick ass-kissers with you massacred the Hightower family. I'm also going to prove that it's you pus buckets who are 'haunting' this valley and killing innocent people to do it."

"Kill me? Is that threat or prophesy?"

The entire saloon knew exactly what Scully was asking. In the States a threat to kill a man was considered rhetoric; in the Territories, however, the threat was the same as an attempt, and the man threatened had the immediate right to kill in self-defense.

Suddenly the air in the bar fairly crackled with tension. The men behind Scully moved out of the ballistics path. Fargo coiled for the draw.

"It's a threat," he replied in a calm, strong voice, "and before too long it will be a fact. Jerk it back if you've a mind to."

Scully was silent for at least ten heartbeats. "Like you said," he finally replied, "maybe you got something I want, and maybe this ain't the best time to kill you. But believe you me, you lanky son of a bitch—it won't be long and you're gonna buy the farm, bull and all."

"That's mighty gaudy patter, all right," Fargo said. "But like you said—the worm *will* turn."

Scully and his companions thumped out of the silent saloon, spurs chinging.

"Didn't even pay for their damn liquor," Skinner groused.

Sitch's knees suddenly gave out on him and he was forced to grab the bar to support himself. "Christ Almighty, Fargo! You were on the feather edge of a shootout with that lethal bastard even after seeing what he did with that poker chip? Why?"

"Because poker chips don't shoot back," Fargo replied, taking a deep slug of his beer and wiping the foam off his mustache. "That's why."

13

The two men retrieved their horses and rode west out of town, avoiding the stage road. Fargo used Ursa Major, the Great Bear, to locate the North Star and get his bearings from the two fixed points.

"What were you looking at in the sky?" Sitch asked. "It just looks like a million stars to me."

"There's likely more than a million," Fargo replied. "That's why you have to know which ones you're looking for. One will take you to a second, and then you're in business. Maybe later I'll show you how to pick out a half dozen or so that can be mighty useful."

"Where we headed?"

"As close as we can get to that clearing we found yesterday, the place Scully is using for all the 'haunting' around here."

Fargo took a good whiff of the cool night air. "Rain's blowing in," he said, "and the wind's picking up—we're in for a storm, but it won't last long in these parts. We need to hurry if we don't want to get soaked and freeze our asses off."

Fargo found a good spot he estimated was about a mile from the clearing. There wasn't much shelter from the gathering wind, but the autumn-cured grass was plentiful and a little seep spring provided clean water.

"The only tree cover is scraggly jack pine," he remarked as the two men dismounted and put their horses on long ground tethers. "We can't stay here very long—the red sashes will have vedette riders out looking for us once they realize we've left town."

As they stripped the leather from their mounts Fargo felt the first wind-whipped drops of rain pelt his face.

"Shit," Sitch cursed. "We're in for a soaking."

"Like hell we are," Fargo replied. "We're gonna make what's called a half-faced camp. Watch and learn, tenderfoot. Get the canvas groundsheet off my blanket roll and the pegs and rawhide whangs rolled up inside it."

Fargo quickly used his Arkansas toothpick to hack a straight branch and two forked branches off the surrounding jack pines. He planted the forked branches firmly in the ground and laid the straight pole in the forks.

"The rain will be driven by the wind," Fargo explained, "so you stretch the canvas out to windward at a forty-five-degree angle. Years ago I put eyelets into both sides of the sheet, and I tie it to the pole with the whangs. Then all I have to do is kick the pegs into the ground securely and tie off the bottom. We'll have plenty of room even with our saddles tossed in with us."

By the time the rain was driving down in sheets, both men were under the shelter. The rain pelted the groundsheet in a steady drumming.

"Snug as two bugs in a rug," Sitch remarked, gnawing on a hunk of jerky. "You know what I really miss, though? Sowbelly and corn bread."

"Good fixin's," Fargo agreed. "We'll be having corn dodgers for breakfast—closest we'll get to corn bread on the trail."

"Fargo," Sitch remarked after a minute of silence, "what was all that business in the saloon about you having something Scully wants?"

"It was a bluff, but it paid off. I've suspected for some time that Scully believes Belle Star, or whoever the hell she really is, has got something Scully wants bad—so bad he's been murdering to get it. I don't know if she does have anything, but I'm hoping Scully will believe I have it and leave her alone."

"Yeah, but what is it?"

"Use your noodle, remember? If there really is anything, my guess would be it's a map or diagram of some kind showing where that silver vein is—something Hightower made before he went bust and had to leave the area around Rough and Ready. But these 'treasure map' deals are usually just saloon lore. I got no idea if Belle really has anything at all, but Scully sure's hell thinks so."

"Yeah, but whether she does or not, why is she staying mum and risking her life? You think maybe it's because she has no idea who the attackers were? If that's so, the law wouldn't know who to go after and she'd be in real danger."

"The way you say. Damned if I know what's going on in that pretty little head of hers. Trying to figure out a woman is like trying to bite your own teeth."

"She's more than just pretty," Sitch said with conviction. "She's got sprites in her eyes like no woman I've ever seen. She's got the flame within her, that gal has."

"The hell are you all of a sudden— a poet?"

"Nope. But I think you're gonna get lucky and trim her, Fargo. And when you do, you're going to find her to be one hot little firecracker."

"That'd be hunky-dory with me. But somehow I doubt that I'll ever find out. I don't exactly stand in thick with her."

"Yeah, well, I don't doubt it one bit," Sitch insisted. "And for such a great Romeo of the range, you're reading her all wrong."

"Oh, I am, huh? And I imagine you're about to enlighten me?"

"Sure. See, when a woman is just indifferent to a man, he hasn't got a chance to bed her unless maybe he's rich and she's a gold digger. But when a woman appears to go out of her way to despise a man, like Belle is treating you, he's already got her stirred up."

Fargo considered that notion and realized Sitch was on to something—many a beautiful lass who had snooted the Trailsman at first had ended up writhing beneath him in sexual ecstasy. But he was reluctant to admit that a homely cuss like Sitch McDougall might be right.

"You know," Fargo replied, "for a jasper who brags he only tops whores, you sure do claim to know plenty about the inner workings of a beautiful woman's mind."

"So what? I know plenty about Paris, too, but I've never been there."

Fargo chuckled in surrender. "Point taken. The lady acts like she's being forced to take nasty medicine every time I get near her. But here's hoping you're right, Mr. Philosopher."

"Damn," Sitch cursed after rummaging in one of his saddle pockets. "I have papers and matches, but I've got out of tobacco."

"I forgot to buy smokes, too," Fargo said. "But root around in my left saddlebag and pull out the little coyote-fur pouch. The stuff inside will make for a pretty good smoke."

Sitch found the pouch and pulled the drawstring to open it, sniffing the contents. "It smells pretty good, but it's not tobacco."

"You think a man riding the high lonesome can always get to stores? You'll get out of plenty of things on the frontier, and you have to learn to find good substitutes. That's red willow bark—go ahead, roll it up."

"It rolls up pretty easy," Sitch admitted.

"You have to strip off the outer bark and then you roast the inner bark good in a fire. Then it pulverizes real easy in your hand and it's ready to smoke."

"Say! It's not got the bite of tobacco, but it's tasty."

"You can substitute for almost anything," Fargo said. "I always run out of salt and pepper, but if you burn the outside of your meat real crisp and sprinkle it with a little gunpowder, there's your salt and pepper taste."

"Yeah," Sitch joked, "but will my ass explode when I fart?"

"If *your* ass explodes," Fargo quipped right back, "all it will do is singe your fancy hat. Listen—the rain has stopped and the wind's dying down. Told you it would just be a quick blow."

Both men stepped outside of the shelter, Fargo watching the sky in the direction of the clearing.

"There!" Sitch said before five minutes had passed. "There's those queer lights again."

Fargo grabbed his tack. "That's all I been waiting for. They're back in that clearing. You wait here—I'm riding in alone to take a squint. I still want to find out about those damn lights."

"You best watch your ampersand, Fargo. If Iron Mike Scully's aim is matched by his speed—"

"No need to finish that sentence." Fargo cut him off, heading out toward his stallion. "You think I'm some simple shit who just landed in Saint Joe with a crate of chickens? I catch your drift."

Fargo knew right where he was headed, and it was a short ride. He held the Ovaro to a canter, the rain-softened ground muffling the hoofbeats. When Fargo figured he was a few hundred yards from the clearing, he walked his stallion in. He swung down and hobbled the Ovaro in a clump of hawthorn bushes about fifty yards from the clearing.

The strange, multicolored lights continued to hover and shimmer over the clearing, reflecting in a wide swath off the low, dense clouds. To cut reflection from his skin, Fargo blackened his face with gunpowder he kept in a flask in his offside saddle pocket. Then he slid his Henry from its saddle scabbard and continued to move in on foot. When he reached the circle of timber he leapfrogged from tree to tree until he was close enough to see the men in the clearing. He folded to his knees to lower his profile.

Their faces were etched in outline by a small fire built aboveground. As he had expected, it was Scully, Romer Stanton and Leroy Jackman. And his suspicion about the weird lights was confirmed when he saw what Jackman was manipulating over the deep fire pit.

It was a so-called "magic lantern" of the type sometimes used by theaters and dance halls, but much larger than any Fargo had ever seen. A large glass bottle was divided into several compartments, each one filled with a different colored oil. Jackman held this one over the fire pit while Stanton worked the bellows to keep the fire burning bright.

Each time Jackman rotated the bottle, the brightly reflected colors changed. When he spun it quickly, the colors overhead turned into a melting and shifting rainbow, a ghostly phantasmagoria that could be seen all over the valley—and especially by the miners at nearby Rough and Ready.

"All right, boys," Scully said. "That's enough haunting for tonight."

Jackman put the magic lantern into a canvas sack, then

shimmied up a tree and tied it to a high branch—explaining why Fargo had missed it during his search.

"We've already driven off more than half of the camp," Romer said in a self-satisfied voice. "And that stunt me and Leroy got planned should flush out enough to shut down the whole shivaree. The rest will have to pull out, and that'll leave just us sashes."

"Sure," Scully replied, "but will we have nothing but our dicks in our hands? All this work ain't worth spit withouten we get that damn map. I'm wondering now if we shouldn't've let Hightower live. Leastways we'd a got something even after giving him half the profits."

"You really think Fargo's got it, boss?"

"The fuck you think I am, a soothsayer? He could be bluffing, all right. But by his talk tonight at the Sawdust Corner, he sure seems to know we're after something."

Jackman had climbed down from the tree and now brushed off his trousers. "Yeah, but if he's got it, he had to get it from the woman. And we ain't even sure that new singer is Dora Hightower."

Scully hawked up a wad of phlegm and spat it out. "That's her, all right. You boys seen how she acted when we asked her to sing another song. And lookit how Bob Skinner clammed up when I asked him about her."

"I string along with Romer," Leroy said. "I just ain't so sure she gave the map to Fargo—Christ, it's worth a fortune."

"Why not give it to him?" Scully reasoned. "She's just a dumb frail like all pretty skirts. She'd turn to the big hero to protect her."

"Jever see a bitch that good-lookin'?" Romer put in. "She hits you right bang in the eye and then right bang in the pecker. Man, what I'd give to have her playing bucking bronco on my rodeo pole."

Scully cursed. "You assholes are worried about fleas while tigers are eating us alive. Forget the poon, wouldja? It's Fargo and that damn map we got to worry about. I near-bout burned him down in the saloon tonight, boys. But the thought of that map stayed my hand."

"Yeah, and see, he *knew* you were a better shootist," Leroy said. "I ain't trying to cross you, Iron Mike, but don'tcha see why he mighta made up that shit about having something you want? He said it on account he knows you could put six holes in his liver before he even cleared leather—twelve if you jerked back both of those Navies."

Fargo watched Scully suck in his cheeks, mulling the idea. Leroy's kiss-ass flattery calmed Scully's voice when he replied.

"Naw . . . you boys are missing the point. Of course Fargo knows he can't win a call-down with me— ain't no man in the territory could do that. But if it was all swamp gas, why *that* partic'lar claim? Why would he know we're looking for anything at all unless the bitch at least told him about the map?"

Leroy looked at Romer. "Yeah, we didn't think of that."

"That's why I do the thinking," Scully said. "You boys are good men, but you ain't got the mentality to figure the percentages and angles."

"Mike," Romer said, "I been wondering about that pasty-faced fop siding Fargo. Man alive, he cracks a mean whip! I never seen the like in all my born days."

"Damn straight," Scully agreed. "But he's gotta get in close to be dangerous with it, and nothing's faster'n a bullet."

"When I rode up to Virginia City and paid off Linse Lofley to put that story in the newspaper," Leroy said, "he told me about that little cockchaser. He was with a medicine show, doing whip tricks. Lofley said he got into a poker game with Big Ed Shack and that bunch Ed hangs with, and they caught the runt cheating. But somehow that little shit got away, stole a horse and lit a shuck out of town."

"I'll be damn," Scully said. "Big Ed is about half rough, all right. If that soft-handed bastard done all that maybe we been selling him short, boys. Fargo don't seem like the type to take on a sidekick that wouldn't be of no use to him."

Fargo, who had been concentrating close on this conversation, didn't hear the slithering in the leaves beside him until it was too late. A sudden weight moving onto the back of his legs and then stopping, however, turned his stomach into a ball of ice.

This area was crawling with rattlesnakes. There were plenty of harmless snakes, too, but at the moment Fargo was literally in no position to find out. The slightest movement to grab either his gun or the toothpick in his boot would trigger a bite, and on his knees like this, the bite would be high up and closer to the heart—greatly increasing the chances of death if it was a rattler.

Fargo knew exactly why the snake had halted, and now sweat was pouring freely from under his hatband. The reptile was flicking its tongue rapidly to gather odor particles and identify this new object. There were only two outcomes possible: it would strike or it would flee. His only option was to remain as still as a marble statue and await his fate.

Seconds seemed to become hours and Fargo hoped his suddenly racing pulse wouldn't be detected by the snake. If it was a rattler and it chose to bite him, it would almost certainly be in a spot Fargo couldn't get at to suck out the poison.

He held his breath until it felt as if his lungs would burst, wondering if this was the night when he had finally reached the end of his trail. Then relief washed over him when the weight moved across his legs and the snake slithered away to his right.

By now the three killers in the clearing had kicked dirt over their ground fire and smothered the flames in the deep pit by throwing a coat over it. They slipped the hobbles off their horses and rode out in the direction of Rough and Ready.

Fargo headed back toward the Ovaro, Scully's incriminating remark burning into his thoughts like a hot branding iron: *I'm wondering now if we shouldn't've let Hightower live.*

That was all Fargo needed to hear. He was already working out a plan. Tomorrow he would ride into Carson City and talk to Sheriff Vance. This deal the Trailsman was caught up in would have to be fought just like a war: one battle at a time. But unlike a war, he had to win every battle, and right now the odds were heavily stacked against him.

14

Fargo kicked Sitch McDougall awake while the sun was still a bloodred blush on the eastern horizon.

"What the hell?" Sitch complained, rubbing the rough crumbs of sleep from the corners of his eyes. "Another hour of sleep wouldn't hurt."

"It could hurt real bad," Fargo said, "if we get caught out in the open like this. We'll need to find a more secure campsite. But for now tuck some grub into your belly and then tack your horse. We're riding back into Carson City."

"We just left," Sitch pointed out as he struggled to get his boots on. "Why didn't we just stay at the livery again?"

"I'm making the medicine, remember? And you're taking it. Just do what I tell you."

"All right, but what about the hot coffee and corn dodgers you said we were gonna have this morning?"

"The wood's too wet, dunderhead."

Sitch had been sound asleep when Fargo returned to camp the night before. Now, while the two men had a quick meal of hardtack and dried fruit, Fargo filled him in on the revealing conversation he had overheard at the clearing as well as the source of the "ghost lights."

"And I heard Scully confirm that the sashes massacred the Hightower family," Fargo concluded. "I never really doubted it, but it's good to hear it from the horse's mouth."

"Sure. But why are we going back into town?" Sitch pressed.

"My word about all this haunted-valley hogwash isn't worth a plugged peso, that's why. I need to take witnesses out to that clearing."

After a rushed meal both men saddled their mounts. Even

this early, Fargo could feel the gathering heat—the day was going to be a scorcher. Before he put the saddle blanket on, he unrolled a gunny sack to put under it.

"What's that for?" Sitch asked.

"It's cooler than the wool blanket."

Fargo had also copied Mexicans and equipped his saddle with a hair girth about five inches wide to avoid chafing his stallion. Sitch watched him cinch it.

"You sure do seem to coddle that horse," he remarked.

"Balls. A horse, like a gun, is a tool. You don't 'coddle' a gun when you keep it clean and oiled—you want to make sure it saves your life when you need it."

Sitch nodded. "Sure. I'm remembering all this, Fargo. I've already learned enough from you to fill up a book."

Fargo snorted but let that pass without comment. The two men hopped their horses and headed east toward Carson City.

They found the sheriff sleeping in one of the cells. Fargo woke him up and described everything he had seen and heard in the clearing the night before, although he didn't connect the missing Dora Hightower to the new saloon singer.

"So Scully admitted it?" Vance said, swinging his feet out onto the floor and wrestling his boots on. "Came right out and said they done the massacre?"

"Yeah, but it means nothing without a second witness. My word against his."

"It means plenty to me though. I believe every word you said."

"Speaking of witnesses—I need at least two to ride back out there with me, Sheriff," Fargo concluded. "Your word alone won't be enough—there's too many here in town who already think you shouldn't have pinned that badge on me. We need somebody who's likely to be believed."

Sheriff Vance nodded, stood up and stretched, then buckled on his gun belt.

"Well, there's Otis Mumford. He puts out the *Carson City Messenger*, our weekly newspaper. But he ain't like that crooked bunch that does the *Territorial Enterprise* up in Virginia City."

"Otis Mumford, huh?" Fargo mulled that. He had read an

issue of the *Messenger* while eating in a café, and it was far less flamboyant and sensational than the Virginia City newspaper. "Can he ride?"

"After a fashion," Cyrus Vance replied. "He's only got a buggy, but it's pulled by a combination horse that old Peatross broke to saddle or traces. The trouble is, he ain't exactly what you'd call a courageous fellow. Then again, he don't care one whit for them red sashes. He's attacked them in print, and that takes some courage. I reckon that's why Scully's men had to ride to Virginia City to get that pack of lies in print. But I don't figure Otis would be too keen to ride that close to Rough and Ready. Still . . ."

The sheriff rubbed his stomach and belched as he conned it over. "Still, he does dearly love a good story and he's what you might call a crusader. You boys wait here while I go talk to him. I'll have to pick up some milk from Ma Kunkle, too. My gut feels like there's a bonfire inside it."

Twenty minutes later the sheriff returned with Otis Mumford in tow. The newspaperman had a craggy, nut-brown face so emaciated that the flesh was drawn knuckle-tight over his prominent cheekbones. Silver-white hair flowed around his head like a wild mane.

"Mr. Fargo," he said after the two men were introduced, "I never for one moment believed that ridiculous broadsheet claiming you massacred the Hightower family. I suspected Scully and his fellow criminals from the moment I heard about it. Proving this 'haunted valley' nonsense won't exculpate you from that charge, of course."

"It won't," Fargo agreed, forced to guess what "exculpate" meant. "But it should start people thinking and put some heat on that greasy sack outfit. I 'preciate you agreeing to ride out with us. You gents ready?"

Mumford was obviously a timid man, and Fargo saw his Adam's apple bob hard as he swallowed nervously. But he gamely nodded. "It's my duty as a newspaperman."

They waited while the sheriff, his face wrinkled in disgust, took down two glasses of milk. Fargo stayed alert for trouble on the ride out, but it proved uneventful. He showed both men the megaphone, the bellows, the fire pit and shinnied up the tree to retrieve the magic lantern.

"Well, damn my eyes," Vance said. "It still don't explain them blood-sucked corpses, though."

"Nothing to explain," Fargo replied. "They were just more murder victims. Look here—"

Fargo pulled a sharp awl from a saddle pocket. He often used it with buckskin string to repair his boots, clothing and tack.

"You knock a man unconscious," he explained, "and then run anything with a sharp point like this into the jugular twice so it looks like bites. If you've ever seen a man whose throat was sliced, you know they turn chalk white when they bleed out."

"I'm convinced, Mr. Fargo," Mumford said sincerely. "But I have to report that it was you who found all this, and I assume you know what that means?"

"Yeah, that I did all the haunting crap myself."

"I can vouch that he didn't," Sheriff Vance put in. "This has been going on steady for months. I know for a fact, from army telegrams, that Fargo has spent the last three months as an express messenger between Fort Churchill and Camp Floyd. The army logs in the time that every message is sent and received. He couldn't possibly have been doing all this spooky shit in Carson Valley and carrying out his duties at the same time."

"Excellent," Mumford said. "But that leaves one other possible accusation that must be eliminated—the possibility that Mr. Fargo planted all of this evidence, which of course I don't believe. But I have an obligation to—"

"I notice you're not one for reading sign, Mr. Mumford," Fargo cut him off. "Look around you. Notice how packed flat the ground is. Look at all the different boot prints and hoofprints. Look over there at the edge of the clearing where they hobble their mounts—look at all the droppings. Some are fresh, others are so old they're like baked clay."

"Just so," the journalist said, clearly satisfied. "The moment we get back to town I'm going to put my printer's devil to work setting the type. There'll be a special edition out this very day with broadsheets all over town."

"I'm wondering," Sheriff Vance said. "Should we destroy all this equipment now? Or should I keep it as evidence?"

"I'd keep it in your office," Sitch suggested. "It would take them time to replace it, especially the magic lantern. If the haunting stops right after Mr. Mumford's newspaper story, that'll just make it more obvious that the story is accurate. And if by some chance this deal gets brought before that circuit judge you mentioned, the evidence might help."

The sheriff cast a speculative glance at the horse thief and card cheat. "Ask a crook to catch a crook, huh? Son, if you ever go straight you might make a good lawman."

"My digestion is bad enough, Sheriff, and I see how yours has become. If I'm going to risk my life, it'll have to be for better profit than thirty dollars a month."

Fargo said nothing to this "circuit judge" business, but he had a different form of justice in mind. Scully and his cronies had not only intended to hang him, they had beaten him when he was tied up. And far worse, they had slaughtered an innocent family, parents and young daughters alike.

I'm wondering now if we shouldn't've let Hightower live. Scully's words picked at Fargo's memory like a burr under a saddle as the men mounted up. The only law now would be gun law, and Fargo intended to be judge, jury and executioner.

Otis Mumford was as good as his word. By late afternoon broadsheets were plastered up all over town, the lead headline blaring in huge print:

"HAUNTED VALLEY" PROVED A HOAX!!!

Citizens had gathered in clumps all over town to read it. Fargo had already read it. Although Mumford was forced to cite Fargo as the original discoverer of the evidence in the clearing, he made it clear that Mumford himself and the sheriff had witnessed it and mentioned the overwhelming proof that Fargo couldn't have done it—and that signs in the clearing proved a group of men had been gathering there for some time.

Mumford, more ethical than his reckless and crooked newspaper peers in Virginia City, did not overtly mention the names of Mike Scully, Romer Stanton and Leroy Jackman even though Fargo had caught them red-handed. He did, however, remind the public that the chief result of the phony haunting was to drive away silver miners who did not wear red sashes. He also suggested that the haunting might well be tied into the massacre of the Hightower family.

Fargo was no fool and realized the newspaperman had placed himself in jeopardy. He and Sitch stopped by Mumford's little cubbyhole office to thank him for his courage.

"I talked to the sheriff," Fargo said. "He agrees with me that you should bunk with him for a few days just to play it safe. I guarantee you it won't be that long before you'll have nothing to worry about with Scully."

Relief swept over Mumford's emaciated face. "I will indeed do that, Mr. Fargo. As you of course already know, the Pony Express went bankrupt just last month—not coincidentally, just as the transcontinental telegraph was completed. Even though we still don't have any railroads west of the Missouri River, Carson City is now linked to the Associated Press telegraphic dispatch system. I sent this story out to the entire country. There's been the usual sensational interest in this haunted valley nonsense, and I'm certain newspapers all over the States will pick up this story. I've no doubt Scully will be outraged even though he's not directly accused."

"Outraged," Fargo agreed, "and maybe just a little bit nervous, too. But this thing has to be brought to a head. You just make sure you stick with the sheriff—he may have a weak stomach, but he's a former Texas Ranger and recommendations don't come much higher than that."

"Are we riding out to set up our next camp?" Sitch inquired as the two men emerged back outside on the boardwalk.

"What did I tell you yesterday?" Fargo snapped.

"Oh. Yeah, that's right. We don't make camp until after dark. And it's still a couple hours until sundown."

"Long as we got time to kill, might's well do it in the Sawdust Corner."

"Ahh . . . you're gonna arrange another tryst with that buxom brunette, huh?"

Fargo grinned at the memory of Libby Snyder and that loudly rustling cornhusk mattress. "Pleasant as that would surely be, old son, it's a pretty blonde I'll be working on—and not to get under her petticoats."

The moment the two men entered, Fargo's eyes moved quick as lassos, watching every part of the saloon for trouble. But if anything, the hostility toward him and Sitch seemed to have lessened. A few men still glowered at them, but most simply ignored the pair. Fargo liked being ignored—liked it just fine.

Otis Mumford's news story, Fargo surmised. Even though it had nothing directly to do with Fargo's supposed cold-blooded murder of an innocent family, it had gotten a few men thinking about the red sashes and exactly what they might be up to.

Bob Skinner greeted the two men at the bar. He drew a beer for Fargo. Then he looked at Sitch, grinned broadly, and proffered a bottle of Very Old Pale, his best whiskey stock.

"Essence of lockjaw?" he asked the whip master.

"What, at six bits a pop? Surely you jest, bar dog?"

"On the house—take the whole bottle. That whip show you put on last night got my customers so excited they ordered extra drinks."

"Nix on the entire bottle," Fargo cut in. "He can have two jolts, Bob, and that's it. If you let him get snockered, you might be killing him."

"Now I got a nursemaid," Sitch grumbled.

"Anyhow," Bob said, "if Fargo doesn't get you killed, son, I'll hire you on anytime. Ten bucks a week and found, and you can have as many free whacks as you want at the doves topside."

Fargo glanced at Sitch and scowled. "You little shit. I've never had a job offer like that."

Bob placed both hands atop the bar and leaned closer to Fargo. "Listen . . . I had a little talk with Belle about you. I don't know that it did much good, but I suggest you have another dance with her."

Fargo brightened at this news. Bob slipped him a few free dance tickets. Fargo headed toward the dance floor, but he ended up dancing with Libby first when she deserted her partner and grabbed Fargo.

"Well," she greeted him in a teasing lilt, "looks like I'm the third button on a two-button shirt."

"I'm not good at riddles, lass."

"I'm talking about Miss Belle Star. Looked to me like you two were getting a bit chummy during that last dance you had."

"Chummy? If the woman was any colder I'd have frost-bitten hands."

"It just looks that way. She's starting to relent, as the lady novelists say. But your only interest is in *protecting* her, right?"

"Right. That and getting some information from her."

Libby tossed back her head and laughed as Fargo spun her around. "Oh, I'm sure you'll get something from her, all right. Must be all that lavender water she splashes on her bodice."

"You smell mighty fragrant too, Libby."

"You go ahead and have your fun with her, Skye. Why shouldn't you? But you be careful. Something about that gal just doesn't tally. I'm sure you can handle yourself against any man in the country. But a beautiful woman . . . that's a different kind of danger."

Libby returned to her original partner and Fargo crossed to stand in the line of men waiting to dance with Belle. To his surprise, she accepted his ticket first. His surprise intensified when she gave him a pearly white smile that would have dazzled a dead man.

"Well, now," he said, "I must've gotten rid of my cooties."

"Bob spoke to me about you. As he put it: 'Fargo is a right decent sort.' I apologize for treating you so badly."

"I figure you've got your reasons, lady."

Her smile faded. "Oh, you can say that again. But this is no place to talk. Bob's been letting me stay in a room at the back of the saloon—it's behind the one girls use for changing clothes. But I don't want you seen coming through the door. There's a window that opens onto the alley behind the saloon. If I leave it open a crack, will you come to see me at eleven p.m.? That's when my shift ends."

Fargo had crawled through many windows to meet women—and even crashed through the glass of several on his way out, just ahead of a load of buckshot.

"You can count on it," Fargo assured her. He had been tempted to add the name "Dora" to the end of his remark, but they were getting along too well to risk spoiling it now.

He finished the dance and headed toward the bar again. The sudden sea change in her attitude toward him had, at first, elated Fargo. But Libby's warning just now came back to him in full force: *Something about that gal just doesn't tally.*

15

At the eastern edge of the silver-mining camp called Rough and Ready ran a quick-flowing creek that originated in the nearby Sierra Nevada. While Skye Fargo was killing time before his eleven p.m. meeting with Belle Star, three miners—Junebug Clark, Ron Bursons and Dennis Moats—were watering work mules in the creek.

The autumn wind had turned cold not long after sundown, howling through the sierra passes with a ghostly moaning that had all three men on edge. The strange, inexplicable lights, the gruesome screams, the blood-sucked corpses of the past few months had taken their toll on the miners' fortitude, and now the shadows cast by rafts of clouds blowing across the moon seemed sinister and threatening. None of the miners at Rough and Ready had yet heard about Otis Mumford's latest story.

"Boys," Junebug said, "I don't know how much longer I can hang on. We ain't pulling out enough ore to do much except lay in supplies. I'm thinking about heading up to the Comstock and working for one of the big companies. I hear they're hiring on men for the Big Virginia Mine."

"Yeah, but you won't put nothing by against the future there, neither," Moats pointed out. "You'll bust your nuts from can to can't for a dollar fifty a day. And them big corporation boys don't provide food nor shelter."

"The rich man's always dancing," Bursons added, "while the poor man pays the band. But leastways they ain't got no walking dead thereabouts."

"You got *that* right," Moats admitted. "But won't be long and we won't have enough men left here to keep us going."

While the mules tanked up, all three men flopped onto

their bellies to drink the delicious cold water. Thus occupied, they didn't notice when a pale, ghostly figure on horseback materialized from the surrounding pine trees.

The chinking of a bit ring and the snuffling of the horse made them sit up and turn around. The pale-butter moonlight revealed an unsettling sight: the lone figure in the saddle was draped in white with his hat pulled low to cover most of his face.

"Evening, gents," the mysterious rider called out in a hoarse, oddly labored voice.

"Guh-good evening," Junebug responded, his own voice reedy with fright.

Something banged into the ground near Junebug's feet—a five-gallon bucket.

"Fill that bucket to the rim and hand it up to me," the ghost rider commanded.

"Sh-sh-sure," the miner replied, hastily rising to his feet to carry out the order. He dipped the bucket into the creek and moved forward a few paces to hand it to the rider.

All three of them stared, their fear and wonder deepening in the wan moonlight, as the ghostly shape hoisted the heavy bucket onto his shoulder with a mighty grunt and tipped it to drink. They turned numb with disbelief as the white-shrouded figure steadily dipped and guzzled, taking no break and draining the entire contents without spilling a drop.

Loudly, he smacked his lips and threw the empty bucket back down. "I thankee, boys. That's the first drink I've had since the Paiutes done for me. *And you get mighty damn thirsty in hell.*"

As mysteriously as he had appeared, the ghost rider faded into the dark mass of surrounding trees.

Junebug's knees gave out and he sank back to the ground. His breath came fast and hard, as if he'd just run a great distance. An icy coating of shock froze each man in place. It was Moats who spoke first, his mouth so dry his tongue felt like a corn husk.

"You seen it too, boys, right?"

"We seen it," Junebug affirmed after swallowing hard to find his voice. "You heard him—he was one of them that was slaughtered in this valley back in fifty-eight."

Ron Bursons, a Catholic, made the sign of the cross. "By the Virgin! Boys, we're damn lucky he didn't suck out our blood! Junebug's right—I'm pulling up stakes tomorrow and putting this place behind me for good."

"God strike me dead if I ever seen anything to top it," Romer Stanton boasted. "I'd wager a purty them three shit their pants."

"'You get mighty damn thirsty in hell!' Romer, you sly bastard," Leroy Jackman praised, "it was a corker. I was close enough to hear and see everything. Junebug is a sorta leader among the men since Duffy Beckman lit out. When the word gets out to the rest, they'll all bust loose from these diggin's faster'n you can spit."

Romer made a grand production of removing the sheet covering him to reveal the cow bladder wrapped around his body. Its mouth was stretched tight onto a funnel that rested under the sheet near his right shoulder. Jackman went into fits of laughter while Romer disencumbered himself.

"Oh, Lu-lu girl!" Jackman said between sputtering laughter. "Romer, you outdone yourself with that one!"

"You two chuckleheads can quit taking bows right now," Iron Mike Scully snapped. "Have you already forgot about that broadsheet that was pasted up all over Carson City today? It's a damn good thing we had Caswell watching the town or *we* wouldn't even know about it. If the men catch wind of it, there goes the whole shebang."

"They won't, boss," Romer said confidently. "My little act knocked all three of those boys into the middle of next Sunday. They'll light a shuck out of here tomorrow morning before the dew dries off the grass. And the rest will go with them."

"They might at that," Iron Mike conceded. "It was a good plan, Romer."

The three men had avoided their usual clearing now that it had been exposed, meeting in dense trees just beyond the creek.

"But here's the way of it," Iron Mike added. "Since that poncy Otis Mumford wrote that story, time is nipping at our asses, boys. He done everything except say flat-out that we're behind all the haunting—not to mention the killing of the Hightowers. We got no equipment now, and those cheese dicks in town are going to see that all the lights and shit has stopped."

"That's the straight," Jackman said, the joviality deserting his voice. "They'll see that Mumford was right. That'll get them all lathered against us once they start wondering about the family being killed. It's gonna get hot for us, 'specially with Fargo still around egging it all on."

"Now you're whistling," Scully said. "We got no choice now but to lay hands on that map, and quick. And I'm still thinking that Dora Hightower gave it to Fargo."

"But even if we manage to kill Fargo," Romer said, "he ain't likely to be carrying it around. And once we put him under, there goes our last hope for a fortune in silver. Even if we get the map, we'll have to clear out for a while and let things settle down in the valley."

"That's how I see it too," Scully agreed. "So the big idea is, we *don't* kill Fargo. We capture him and put the screws to him—hard. Sure, he's tough—tough as rawhide. But even the toughest hombre has a breaking point if you put him under enough of the right kind of pain."

"I ain't so sure of that where Fargo is concerned," Jackman gainsaid. "From what I hear, he's been tortured before—even by Comanches, and those red devils have made an art of inflicting pain."

"All true," Scully conceded. "But if a red-hot nail shoved up his pee pee hole don't do it, there's one thing that will—taking that blond bitch prisoner and torturing *her* right in from of him. He's one a them 'noble' sons of bitches, and he won't watch a woman being tortured to death."

"I'll give you all that," Jackman said. "But we don't know where Fargo *or* the bitch is staying."

"No, but we know where the skirt is working. If we have to, we'll snatch her right out of the saloon. That would be a last resort, though, on account there'd be too many witnesses. She has to be staying in town somewheres—we got to find out where. We know Fargo and the whip boy stopped boarding their horses at the livery, so they must be camped in this area. We can't give up looking for them neither."

"It's a tall order, boss," Romer said. "The bitch we can prob'ly take. But going after Fargo would be like strolling into a lion's den."

Scully twirled both ivory-gripped Navy Colts from their holsters. "You boys seen me gun down Dirty Don Bodner in Santa Fe. And Frank Winkler in El Paso. Both them fuckers was talked up big and had notches all over their barking irons. You really think I can't send Fargo to his ancestors?"

"Hell, he won't even clear leather before you pop him over," Jackman said. "But we still have to find him first."

Shortly after eleven p.m., while Sitch was putting on another trick-whip show in the saloon, Fargo slipped around into the alley behind the Sawdust Corner.

Still not completely trusting the blond beauty who called herself Belle Star, Fargo hunkered low in the chilly night wind, studying the alley in both directions. Packing crates were stacked everywhere, and a few buckboards behind neighboring businesses provided plenty of good ambush nests.

He had left his Henry with Sitch. Fargo shucked out his Colt and approached a well-lighted window in a deep crouch. The window was cracked open a few inches.

"Belle," he called in a loud whisper over the sill, "it's Fargo. Can you hear me?"

"Yes," her low, musical voice called back. "Why don't you come in?"

"I will, but turn down the wick on that lamp until I'm inside."

Fargo had no intention of brightly outlining himself during the vulnerable few seconds he would need to climb inside. The yellow glow inside faded to near darkness and Fargo slid the window wide open, vaulting over the sill. He closed the window, drew the monk's cloth draperies closed over it, then stepped to one side and tucked at the knees.

"All right, lady," he said, his Colt still to hand, "turn up the light."

A milk-glass lamp glowed bright, pushing the shadows back into the corners and revealing a sight that made Fargo forget to take his next breath. Belle Star—who he was now certain was in fact Dora Hightower—stood near an iron bedstead, its mattress covered with a thick eiderdown quilt.

Her unrestrained tresses flowed like a waterfall over her shoulders, and she wore a thin silk peignoir that was as transparent as a fly's wing. Fargo could easily see the dark circles of her nipples, the thatch of hair on her mons, and hourglass hips under a trim waist on which a corset would have been wasted. It all meshed wonderfully with her gorgeous, fine-boned face.

That silk thingamabob, Fargo thought, and all her fine dresses—Bob Skinner was obviously head over heels to lay out that kind of money on fancy feathers.

She stared at his Colt. "Are you afraid of me?" she asked in a lilting tease.

"I'm always extra careful when I scout new territory," he quipped, leathering his shooter.

"Yes, I suppose that's how men of your reputation stay alive. Bob told me all about you and spoke very highly of your character. That's why I invited you here."

Fargo had a vastly different idea about why she had invited him into her hideout room, and it wasn't just so that she could seduce him—which she obviously was. She was using her sexual favors as a bribe, but Fargo wasn't stupid enough to bring that up right now—not with a throbbing erection turning the front of his buckskins into a pup tent. The right kind of bribe was fine by him.

Belle couldn't possibly miss the proof of his arousal. Her voice suddenly went husky. "My stars and garters! You certainly are ready, aren't you?"

Fargo unbuckled his gun belt and opened his fly, letting her see in more detail exactly how ready he was. For several long moments she appeared speechless.

"I heard some tittering among the girls after Libby whispered some things about you," she finally said. "Now I know what they were talking about."

She stood up and pulled the peignoir over her head, stretching out on the bed. Again Fargo marveled at the ivory smooth skin. For such a slim girl her breasts were impressive—hard, round, and high-thrusting, with rose nipples that she began tweaking to tease him.

"Some men have called me delicate," she told him as he crossed to the bed, "but I like it when a man takes me hard and fast. And you look just like the type of man to do that."

"With me it's always the woman's call," Fargo assured her as he parted her creamy smooth thighs and mounted his favorite saddle.

Fargo lined his manhood up with her nether portal and thrust into her hard, opening wide a silk-lined tunnel of explosive pleasure. She cried out and clawed into his back as Fargo drove into her just the way she had requested—hard and fast. She keened repeatedly as climaxes washed over her, bending and raising her legs until the well-turned ankles were locked behind his shoulders.

At this furious clip Fargo's first, violent release didn't take long. But his manhood never softened and he kept right on driving into her until a second, massive release left both of them panting for breath in a confused moil of arms and legs.

"Skye Fargo," she finally managed, "you're not a man— you're a savage stallion."

"Thanks for the compliment . . . Dora," he replied as he sat up on the bed for a long, appreciative look at the sated beauty.

She paled slightly and, suddenly self-conscious, pulled one edge of the quilt over her. "There you go again. I've already told you that my real name is Samantha Urbanski."

Fargo emitted a long, weary sigh. "Lady, don't you think it's about time we bury this dog? And I s'pose you're a blonde too, right?"

"Of course, unless you think this is a wig."

"It's a nice dye job, sure. But you made one big mistake."

Fargo slid one hand under the quilt and slid it down to cup her velvet-smooth pubic mound. "When you dyed the hair on your head, you forgot about this soft mat right here. I've been with plenty of blondes, and the hair down below is usually just a shade or so darker than the hair on their head. Yours is a dark copper color—a close match to the hair on the head of the woman I saw fleeing the massacre scene."

She opened her mouth to reply, but his observation had blindsided her and no good lie was forthcoming. Finally: "I didn't expect anyone would be seeing it," she admitted.

"So let's quit playing ring-around-the-rosy about who you are," Fargo said. "Why in the hell are you snowing everybody?"

For a moment Fargo saw her eyes shift toward a chest of drawers in the nearest corner—and a little felt-covered box atop it.

"Skye, I swear by all things holy—I can't tell you anything. I just *can't.*"

"That's why you decided to invite me in here, isn't it? With Bob Skinner, all it took to buy his silence, and get room and board and a complete wardrobe, was some batting of those beautiful eyelashes. But you figured you'd need the heavier artillery to bewitch me into playing along."

"Yes," she admitted. "But after what you just did to me with that heavy artillery of yours, I don't regret that my stratagem has obviously failed. And I see that you were crafty enough to play along until after you got what you wanted."

Fargo grinned. "Of course. If I'm gonna get tossed out of a restaurant, I'll make sure I have my dessert first."

She smiled at his candor; then her pretty face went serious. "All right, so you know I'm Dora Hightower. You already figured that out before tonight. What is it you want from me?"

His brow compressed with sudden puzzlement. "What do *I* want? Christ, Dora, exactly the same thing you should want. You know damn well, don't you, that it was Iron Mike Scully and his men who attacked your family?"

Again she glanced toward that felt box atop the dresser. Then she turned her face away from him.

"Yes," she confessed. "Before I managed to escape in the darkness and hide in the rocks, I heard one of his men call out his name."

"And you mean to tell me that you're willing to just let those murdering scuts wipe out your family and get away with it?"

Now she met his eye, her face a mask of conviction. "They *won't* get away with it. Bob made it abundantly clear to me what manner of man you are. Nothing is going to

119

bring my family back now, but *you* are going to kill those pigs. And that's better than trusting to the law out here. Can you deny that?"

"I'm at least going to kill three of the red sashes," Fargo affirmed, "and any more who get in my way. But you've got to understand, this isn't a story in a penny dreadful. I don't have free rein to kill any man I want to. You were a witness—hell, you were a victim—and a woman's word is rarely doubted in the West. If you come forward on my behalf, nobody will be slapping murder charges on me."

Fargo was deliberately exaggerating the possible trouble he faced from the law. He was more worried about the lies spewed out by the crooked press, and Dora was the key to stopping them.

"Sheriff Vance would never do that," she pointed out.

"No. But there's a crooked magistrate in this town who would require a big payoff to let me off the hook. And a circuit judge who just might sentence me to swing in the breeze. Vance has got no sway over them."

A crystal dollop suddenly formed in her eye and zig-zagged down her cheek, and Fargo didn't think it was just acting.

"Skye, I can't deny a word you've just said. But I beg you—oh, merciful God, I *beg* you to believe me when I tell you it will destroy my life if I reveal myself. It will absolutely destroy me. Do you believe me?"

Fargo studied her for a full thirty seconds in silence. "Yeah, I guess I do. And I'll quit pressing you. Your name is Belle Star."

She suddenly sat up and hugged him hard, sobbing in her relief. "And, Skye, I promise you this—no matter what, I will *not* let you and your friend be framed or sent to the gallows while I sit idly by. If I have to destroy myself and come forward as a witness, I will. But I have faith that Bob is right about you—you're going to take care of this in your own way and no corrupt legal system is going to come after you for it."

Fargo, ever the optimist, patted her shoulder. "Sure, that might well be how things turn out. But listen, something else is nagging at me. I think that little box you've been glancing at might hold something Scully and his bunch are after—something they want with a hell-thirst."

He felt her shoulders stiffen.

"Don't worry," he assured her. "I promised not to press you anymore and I mean it. But you know I'm right. Whatever it is, I've tried to make them think I have it. Maybe they believe that and maybe they don't. Even if they do, there's a good chance they'll try to use you to get it from me. You take my drift, don't you?"

"Oh, do I. I live in fear day and night that they'll figure out where I am."

"Not all criminals are stupid," Fargo said. "By now they've guessed that Bob Skinner knows where you are—and maybe that he's hiding you somewhere in the saloon. It's not safe here for you."

"But where—?"

"I've already figured that out," Fargo assured her. "You won't like it much, but it's the one place in town they'll never think to look for you: the hayloft of Old Man Peatross's livery stable."

"Skye, I couldn't possibly—"

He pressed a finger to her lovely lips, cutting off her objections. "Sure you can. It'll be more comfortable than you think, and I double-damn guarantee it won't be for long. I intend to lance this boil in a puffin' hurry. The next man coming through that window, cupcake, could be Iron Mike Scully. Are you willing to risk that just to have a soft mattress?"

"When you put it that way, no. But when?"

"It has to be tonight or I won't sleep a wink for worrying about you. But this has to be done right. You sit tight while Sitch and me take care of a little business. I know you had a gun when I first saw you because you took a shot at me."

"Skye, I swear I didn't even try to hit you—"

He waved this aside. "I know you didn't. But do you still have it?"

"No. I was in such a blind panic that I somehow lost it while I was hurrying toward Carson City. But I have a little two-shot thing that Bob gave me. He called it a sleeve gun. It's in the top drawer of that chest."

"It's no good to you there. Get it out and keep it to hand until I come back. I'll do four quick taps on the glass to let you know it's me coming back. If anybody touches that window without tapping first, blast him with both shots and then run out into the saloon. While I'm gone, throw together just the things you absolutely need."

"Skye, do you really think the danger is that imminent?"

"Dora," he assured her, "I'm amazed they haven't abducted you already. You're in mortal danger, and every minute we waste is one minute too many."

"Well, aren't you in mortal danger, too?"

Fargo grinned as he rose and buckled on his shell belt. "Sure. But I'm the contrary type who enjoys it."

16

Fargo scrambled back outside through the window. First studying the alley carefully, he returned to the street and entered the saloon through the batwings. He spoke with Bob Skinner for a few minutes, emphasizing the danger Belle Star was in and the need to move her immediately. Knowing that Skinner was hopelessly in love with the woman, Fargo left the distinct impression that she had invited him into the room strictly for a strategy meeting.

"Yeah," Skinner agreed. "It's been nice having her so close by, but I been worried too. Scully seemed mighty interested in that door. Where you moving her to?"

"Would you be offended, Bob, if I don't answer that question? I know you'd never reveal her whereabouts, but it's best if nobody else knows."

The barkeep nodded reluctantly. "I take your point."

"The sashes will likely pump you about where she is. Just act pissed at her. Say she up and quit on you without giving any notice. That's all you know. It's risky for you, Bob, so I'm going to talk to Sheriff Vance tomorrow about keeping a close eye on this place."

By now Sitch had finished his trick-whip show and stood at the bar savoring a glass of top-shelf whiskey.

"Fargo," he boasted, "I made a whopping eighteen dollars when some old buzzard passed the hat. Hell, why have I been wasting my time as a pickpocket and card cheat?"

"That's a sight of money," Fargo agreed. "Give me ten dollars of it."

"What the—? Why should I—?"

"Here we go again. Who *makes* the medicine?"

"You do."

"And who *takes* the medicine?"

"I do."

"All right. Chuck the chinwag and give me ten dollars. It's for a worthy cause."

"Of course it is," Sitch replied sarcastically as he began counting coins onto the bar.

"Now," Fargo said as he pocketed the money, "we got a little job ahead of us. C'mon. We're gonna buttonhole a spy."

As the two men emerged from the saloon into the cold, late-night air, Fargo quickly explained the plan for moving Dora Hightower to the livery stable.

"But Scully is bound to have one of his roaches keeping an eye on us here in town," Fargo said. "We don't want any gunplay—the last thing we need now is for men to come boiling out into the streets. Get that whip of yours ready."

The two men paused in the shadow of an awning, Fargo surveying the main street of Carson City. His attention settled on a lone figure across the street smoking a cigarette, leaning on his back against the front of a dry-goods store.

"I'd say that's our boy," he remarked. "He's smarter than the last two. He's planted himself in the middle of the building so nobody can sneak up on him. Let's go pay our respects."

The two men began crossing the wide, dusty, moonlit street. At first the man had pretended to ignore them. But as they drew nearer in a beeline straight for him, he suddenly flipped his cigarette away in a glowing arc. He moved his hand down toward his holster.

Fargo's Colt leaped into his fist. "Try it, shit heel, and you'll fry everlasting."

"You neen hold that gun on me, mister," the shadowy figure replied as the two men drew nearer. "I ain't done nothing wrong. I just come to town to cut the buck loose a bit."

"You know, Sitch," Fargo remarked, "this town is cram full of maggots."

Now that he was closer Fargo recognized the man by his snakeskin belt and torn rawhide vest—one of the red sashes present at the "trial" out at Rough and Ready.

"You're a liar," Fargo said in a hard-edged voice. "You're part of that murdering trash that lick Iron Mike Scully's ass."

In a lower voice only Sitch could hear, Fargo added: "Get his gun. Then I'll cold-deck the son of a bitch."

With one quick, sharp snap of his whip, Sitch lifted the sidearm from its holster and sent it sliding along the boardwalk.

Fargo followed up quick as an arrow flying from a bow, leaping toward the surprised man and delivering a powerful roundhouse right that sent him staggering to the left. Taking no chances, Fargo followed up with a haymaker that dropped the man in an unconscious heap.

Fargo hooked a thumb toward the chestnut gelding tied off nearby. "That must be his horse. Grab that rope off his saddle horn. And get his gun, too."

Fargo grabbed the man under his armpits and dragged him around the corner of the store. He made short work of trussing him up securely and gagging him tight with the man's filthy bandanna.

"Man alive, Fargo," Sitch remarked, "you were on him so fast he never knew what hit him."

"He'll sure's hell know when he wakes up. C'mon . . . the trickiest part is still ahead of us."

Dora had gathered up her things and tied them inside of a linen sheet by the time the two men returned to her room. Fargo studied the alley carefully before helping her through the window. But he avoided the street and the alley, leading Dora out behind the edge of the town and spiriting her to the livery barn.

"Peatross," Fargo called in a hoarse whisper through the crack between the wide swinging doors. "Can you hear me?"

A moment later, Fargo heard the flat metallic click of a gun being cocked inside.

"Don't shoot me, old roadster," Fargo said. "It's Skye Fargo. Let me in, but don't put up any light until the doors are shut behind me."

Fargo heard the old salt grumbling in a sleep-husked voice and then one of the doors groaned open. Fargo, Sitch and Dora stepped inside the manure-fragrant barn and Fargo swung the door shut.

The scratch of a lucifer lighting, and then a lantern glowed to life. The old hostler stood before them in his dirty long-handles, his sagging, grizzle-bearded face becoming a mask of surprise and embarrassment when he spotted the beautiful woman with them.

"Hell, Fargo, you mighta told me you had a lady in tow. I'd've tossed on some britches."

Dora looked fetching in the flattering, subdued lighting. She wore a simple calico skirt, a knitted shawl, and the ubiquitous coal-shovel bonnet of that era.

"Say, old codger," Fargo said, "any chance this lady could hide out in your hayloft for a spell? It won't be too long."

"A hayloft! This beauty?" Peatross's skinny old arm, corded with veins, lifted the lantern to study her closer. "Why, God's galoshes! Gals like this belong in one a them houses with fancy gingerbread work under the eaves."

"That she does," Fargo agreed. "But things are the way they are, and right now she needs to hide."

"Don't tell me this pretty little filly is on the dodge?"

"She's on the dodge, all right," Fargo said. "But not from the law. Iron Mike Scully and his red sashes are after her."

"Scully! That skunk-bit son of a—"

Peatross caught himself just in time. "You'll have to forgive me, ma'am. I only palaver two languages: American and cussing. Say, you must be Belle Star, that new singer Skinner hired on at the Sawdust Corner. I heard tell how you was mighty easy on the eyes."

Peatross turned his gaze on the Trailsman.

"Fargo, I won't minch the matter. It's any honest man's duty to protect a woman, and this gal can stay here long as she needs to. I got plenty of blankets, and I'll make her comfy as I can. I'm a good cook, and there's always hot coffee and bear sign in the morning," he said, meaning the wildly popular doughnuts shaped like a bear's paw. "But I *don't* want no damn—scuze me, ma'am—dang shootin' war here. I'll hafta pay for any horse caught in the cross fire."

"Don't worry," Fargo assured him. "There's no reason on earth for Scully to think of this place. But just in case . . ."

He took the Volcanic revolver Sitch had whip-lifted from the thug's holster and handed it to Dora. "You've already got that sleeve gun Bob gave you, but that's only good close in.

If anybody comes up that ladder who isn't s'pose to, make it hot for him. And here's ten dollars, old-timer, to take care of food and such. Good luck, Belle. We'll be in touch."

"You two are the ones who'll need luck," she replied. "I feel safe now, but I know you two are in mortal danger."

"Mortal danger?" Peatross repeated, chuckling. "Pretty lady, mortal danger is the street Skye Fargo lives on."

Exhausted from a long day, and with the moon now occluded by thick cloud cover, Fargo didn't use his usual caution when picking a trail camp that night—a decision he would soon come to regret.

The two men had ridden west toward the sierra, Fargo selecting the first location with grass and a little trickle stream. They hastily stripped the leather from their mounts and rubbed them down before placing them on long tethers that allowed them to drink from the stream and graze. Avoiding a fire, they shared a quick meal of jerky and dried fruit, shivering in the cold air.

"I was kinda surprised," Sitch remarked as he gnawed off a hunk of jerky, "when you laid in this grub. Everything I've read about you ballyhoos how you always live off the land."

Fargo snorted. "A man only lives off the land when he's forced to it. You can spend all day hunting and making snares and trotlines and still come up with nothing but the sniffles. Case you haven't noticed, we got more important things to do with our time."

"Me, I'd starve if I couldn't get to a store or trading post."

"Likely you would, especially without a rifle. But except in hard winter weather, a man never needs to starve. I've got by on grass seed, nuts, roots, grasshoppers, lizards and snakes. In the right parts of the West there's always plenty of buffalo bones. The roasted bone marrow is delicious, and you can live on it for weeks."

Using their saddles as pillows, the two men rolled up in their blankets.

"Say, Fargo," Sitch called over to him, "you ought to know this one: what's a bachelor's favorite holiday?"

"You tell me."

"Why, Palm Sunday, of course."

Fargo chuckled. "So far with these jokes of yours you're holding your own."

It took Sitch a few seconds to catch the pun. "That's better than the original joke. I guess I best take myself in hand, huh?"

"You're milking it too far now," Fargo shot back, and both exhausted men broke into laughter at their string of bad puns.

Sitch's voice turned serious. "This gal, Dora—she's hiding two things. Whatever's in that box you mentioned and whatever's got her so scared that she won't even turn in the murderers of her own family. Can you make any sense of it?"

Fargo yawned and pulled his hat over his eyes. "About that box I can take a guess: it's whatever Scully is after, and that's likely a map of some kind her brother made, showing right where that silver vein is s'pose to be. As to the other: it's one helluva stumper to me. She's scared to within an inch of her life about something, and it's not just Scully and his bunch."

"Yeah. Well, I believe her claim that she figures you are going to put paid to the murder of her family. Matter of fact, if I was her I'd be far more likely to leave it to you than whatever law they've got around here. But what—?"

"Put a sock in it," Fargo snapped, his eyelids feeling like they were weighted down with coins.

"On second thought," Sitch corrected himself, "if I was her, the first thing I'd do is strip naked and look at myself in the mirror. Maybe even feel myself up. Say, Fargo, you were back in that room with her for quite a while. Did you—?"

"No, I didn't," Fargo lied. "Now cut the cackle and grab some shut-eye while you can. We're gonna be on the ragged edge for the next couple of days, and this ain't no time to be jacking our jaws about the causes of the wind."

"The ragged edge? What does that—?"

The muffled click of Fargo's hammer sounded from under his blanket.

"Sleep tight," Sitch muttered, rolling onto his side.

17

"Damn it," Fargo cursed when he woke up.

Despite his almost instinctual habit of rising with the sun when he was on the trail, he had overslept this morning by at least two hours. He kicked Sitch awake.

"Stir your stumps, mooncalf. We've got to clear out of here."

Fargo took his bearings. This little clump of juniper and jack pine was a tiny island in a vast surrounding area of scant-grown hills dotted with little growth besides scrub cottonwood and mesquite.

Sitch shook off the last cobwebs of sleep and rose unsteadily to his feet. "Christ, my mouth feels like the last cracker at the bottom of the barrel."

He grabbed his empty canteen and headed toward the little stream. Fargo heard him curse again.

"This damn water is muddy, Fargo! We can't drink this."

"It was good enough for the horses. Just drink it and tack that sorrel. I want to get out of here."

"Well, I'm not a horse. This water—"

"The hell is your major problem?" Fargo snapped, crossing in long strides toward the stream. "Dip your cup in that water then hand me your bandanna."

Fargo folded the bandanna over the mouth of the cup. "This will trap the bigger particles of dirt when you pour it into your canteen. Now drink it and quit bellyaching. We slept too damn late and we need to make tracks. This is a piss-poor defensive position."

Fargo whistled the Ovaro in and was centering his saddle when he glanced to the east and saw it: a yellow-brown dust cloud billowing toward them from behind the surrounding hills.

Sitch followed his gaze and then paled. "Indians?"

Fargo shook his head. "Not likely. They tend to ride in single file to keep the dust down. This is a group of palefaces riding in a wide file—and since there's no soldiers patrolling this area, I'd say it's the red sashes looking for us."

Fargo pulled his field glasses from a saddlebag and studied the area out before them.

"It's sashes, all right. More than I realized Scully controlled, and they're sweeping right toward our position. At least a dozen."

"But how could they know we're here?"

"They don't. It's just our bad luck and my stupidity for sleeping too long. They can't know we're here because they're not even close to the trail we left to get here."

"Maybe they had a rider patrolling and he spotted our horses earlier this morning," Sitch suggested.

Fargo shook his head, lowering the glasses. "A rider couldn't have spotted them through the trees unless he rode right up on them. My stallion wouldn't let a man get that close without waking me up. They decided to sweep the surrounding country to find us, and this just happens to be the direction they picked. I can tell by the way they've fanned out that they're searching, not attacking."

"Well, you told me a man always wants the element of surprise on his side. You're mighty handy with that Henry of yours. Why not just start picking them off?"

"That's not the worst plan in the world," Fargo conceded. "But it's not the best, either. I couldn't possibly wipe that many out of the saddle before they covered down. And then they'd know right where we are. Every man I see has a long gun, and at least some of them are likely good marksmen."

"Then why don't we just run like hell? We've got a jump on them."

"That's not the worst plan, either. My Ovaro can outrun his shadow. But that sorrel of yours is only middling. If they spot us, they'll run you down."

"So how *do* we get the hell out of this fix? Or should we just sit and play a harp?"

"When you can't surprise or mystify your enemy, you mislead him. I know these frontier bullyboys. They're only 'brave' when victory is assured. They'll dump the blanket quick if they think they're heading right toward Indians."

As Sitch opened his mouth to ask yet another damn fool question, Fargo cut him off with a curt order. "Just shut up and do what I tell you. We'll need a big fire, and there's plenty of dry wood lying around here. Gather it up fast. Then get me a big pile of green boughs. We're gonna make Indian smoke. Here, take this."

Fargo handed Sitch his Arkansas toothpick. While Sitch gathered wood and cut boughs, Fargo removed a handful of crumbled bark from a saddle pocket and used small sticks to get a fire started. He carefully laid the larger pieces of wood over it until a good fire was blazing.

"They're close, Fargo," Sitch said with a nervous quaver to his voice. "I can make out Scully now."

Fargo quickly piled the green boughs on, and almost immediately a thick black smoke rose into the morning air. He grabbed his blanket and used it to cover and uncover the billowing smoke.

"What are you signaling?" Sitch asked.

"Prob'ly nothing. I can't read Indian smoke signals, and I don't know one white man who can. But that includes those rat bastards closing in on us."

Fargo's prediction was borne out. The moment the vigilantes band spotted the smoke, they reined in to confer quickly. After less than thirty seconds they reversed their dust and pounded their saddles back toward the east.

"You called it right, Fargo!" Sitch exalted. "They're tearing off like hounds with their asses on fire!"

"Yeah, and we best be the next ones to light out," Fargo said.

"Light out to where?"

"Carson City. I've got to talk to Sheriff Vance about this deal. Dora is reasonably safe now, Sitch, but what about the other girls at the Sawdust Corner? Won't take the sashes long to figure Belle Star is gone, and they're going to figure Libby or one of the others knows where she is. I want some security in that saloon."

Fargo glanced at Sitch's saddlebags and then at Sitch, a sly grin on his face.

"Wait a minute here, Fargo," Sitch protested. "I don't like that scheming look on your face."

"Look, knucklehead, the girls aren't just vulnerable at the saloon. Scully's sewer rats must also know about Ma Kunkle's boardinghouse. So this is where your skills come in."

"Just an everlovin' minute here, I'm not—"

"There, there, that's a tough old soldier," Fargo cut him off. "This will be right up your road."

"The hell are you talking about?"

"I'll tell you after we ride out. There's Bannocks, Shoshones and Paiutes all around this area, and by now some of them must have seen this smoke. It likely makes no sense to any of them, but red aborigines are curious and they *will* be riding this way to puzzle this thing out. I'd just as soon tangle with a she-grizz protecting her cubs—all three of those tribes take special delight in torturing a white man to death, so hop your horse and hop it quick."

Fargo, who always tried to think one step ahead of his enemy, assumed Scully's regulators would know by now that Fargo had thrashed and tied up one of their spies last night.

But he also assumed they would still be watching for him in town. He didn't want them to know that Sitch would soon be in Carson City, so about two miles outside of town he told his companion to wait in a cluster of boulders surrounded by scrub pine.

Fargo remained vigilant as he loped the Ovaro toward town, slowing the stallion to a long trot as he approached the western outskirts. Not sure whether Scully's men had orders to kill or to capture, Fargo carefully studied all the good ambush spots. He paid scant attention to a big hay wagon that rolled away from a feed store at his approach.

The wagon rattled closer, driven by a man in dirty coveralls. The man's floppy hat was pulled low against a bright sun and left the rest of his face in deep shadow. There was nothing unusual about this, and the clay pipe stuck in his teeth further reinforced the familiar image of a poor dirt-scratcher. Fargo knew that a few hardscrabble farms now dotted Carson Valley, providing beef, pork and produce to the thriving boomtown and Virginia City just to the north.

But the rifle on the seat beside the driver caught Fargo's attention—a long-barreled Hawken, hardly the weapon of choice for a farmer.

A Hawken gun, warned a voice somewhere just beneath the level of conscious awareness. *Just like Leroy Jackman carries.*

This thought brought Fargo's focus sharply on the farmer. Danger showed in the lower half of a man's face, the half Fargo could just make out in the shadowed visage. The sudden, determined set of the man's jaw was sickeningly familiar to Fargo.

Fargo's previous thoughts scattered like frightened birds and his mind focused down to nothing but survival. The fine hairs on his nape stiffened, and everything that happened after that took only seconds, but seemed to be slowed down to dream time, as if he were moving underwater and he had become both participant and observer.

"Now!" the driver shouted, tugging rein to swerve the wagon closer to Fargo.

The hay parted to reveal two brawny arms and an ax handle that arced toward Fargo's head in a blur of speed. Because of the split-second warning from his senses, Fargo managed to bring his left arm up to absorb some of the blow. But the impact was still forceful enough to knock him from the saddle as an orange starburst exploded inside his skull.

The Ovaro reared as Fargo flopped into the street. For an eternally long few seconds, Fargo balanced between consciousness and dark oblivion, the life force at some primordial level within him warning that if he passed out all was lost.

Still dazed, he managed to knock the riding thong from his Colt and shuck it from the saddle even as a looped rope settled over his upper body and began to drag him behind the wagon. Fargo shot toward the arms projecting from the hay and heard a yelp of pain as the rope was dropped. The driver whipped the team up even as several weapons opened up, peppering the street all around Fargo with bullets.

Fargo returned several shots into the hay, aiming toward muzzle flash, and a man tumbled out into the street, blood pumping from a bullet hole in his neck. That was all Fargo registered before his head, feeling as if it weighed a ton, suddenly dropped to the ground and the world swirled around him, a loud ringing like hammering on an anvil filling his skull.

18

A voice seemed to be calling him from the end of a long, dark tunnel.

Fargo!

Fargo!

"Fargo! Wake up, son!"

Sheriff Cyrus Vance's voice jarred Fargo back to awareness. "Thank God. I figured you for a goner, Trailsman."

Fargo blinked a few times to get the day in focus again.

"I hustled out as soon as I heard the shooting fray," Vance said. "Can you sit up?"

Fargo's headed throbbed like an abscessed tooth. He saw the sheriff's worried face looking down at him.

"Give me a hand," Fargo replied. "I'm still a little woozy."

"I don't wonder, judging from that swelling on your forehead. I'll fetch my horse from the feed stable—that wagon can't put on much speed."

"Nix on that," Fargo managed as the sheriff helped him to his feet. "That's a damn battle wagon, Cyrus. You'd just be digging your own grave."

The pain was still so sharp that Fargo almost reeled, but he stayed on his feet. He pulled the rope off him.

Sheriff Vance glanced at the body in the street, hands still clutched around the end of the rope. "Well, one man in town is sure fond of you, Fargo—Dave Rohr, the undertaker. Business has picked up considerable since you rode into these parts."

Vance toed a splatter of fresh blood that trailed behind the wagon. "You've killed one and wounded at least one more. I'd wager they left town wiser if not better men. C'mon, let's get you to a doctor."

"No need," Fargo said. "Just help me onto my horse. I need to palaver a little with you."

They returned to the sheriff's office and Fargo gratefully sank into a chair in front of the lawman's desk. Otis Mumford was snoring from one of the jail cells, having followed Fargo's advice to bunk with the sheriff.

"Fargo," Vance remarked as he settled into his swivel chair, "you got the endurance of a doorknob."

Fargo gingerly touched the big knot on his forehead. "Well, damn straight I've got the doorknob, at least. But now I know Scully doesn't want me killed—just captured. Even when they shot at me from the wagon, it was just to suppress my fire—their bullets were deliberately aimed wide of me."

"You know," the sheriff said, removing his hat to whack at flies with it, "I discovered more of your handiwork this morning when I made my early rounds. You dislocated that peckerhead's jaw last night. Doc Templeton snapped it back into joint, and that sash howled like a dog in the hot moons. What, did you hit him with a sledgehammer?"

"Wish I had," Fargo replied. "My right hand's been giving me jip since I hit him."

Fargo noticed a bowl in front of the sheriff filled with some unappetizing looking concoction. He nodded toward it. "I hope that ain't your breakfast."

"You hope wrong. I call it graveyard soup— milk with pieces of bread broken into it. One of the 'solid foods' my stomach can handle. And this vile-smelling brew in the mug is comfrey tea—Ma Kunkle swears it's good for dyspepsia, but it tastes like burro piss. But never mind. . . ."

The sheriff scowled at the bowl and pushed it aside. "I'm more interested right now in something you just said. Why would they want to capture you?"

Fargo knew that he had to bring the sheriff into this deal—all the way in.

"Well, you 'member me telling you about that female witness who escaped from the massacre scene—the one I was searching for?"

The sheriff nodded and Fargo filled him in on everything: that Belle Star was really Dora Hightower, what Scully was almost surely after, and Dora's mysterious refusal to come forward and accuse Scully of the murder of her family—a refusal that had nothing to do with her fear of the vigilantes.

"Thanks for keeping me updated," Sheriff Vance replied sarcastically when Fargo finished. "I hope the presence of a sheriff hasn't inconvenienced you. But, say, what could possibly keep a woman from bringing charges against a bunch of murderers who done that to her family?"

Fargo shrugged a shoulder. "Hell, might's well ask me who teaches kids to play hopscotch? She claims she has faith that I'll handle the matter better than the law can, and maybe she means that. But she couldn't have known about me right away, so what kept her silent so long?"

Vance nodded. "Yeah, and that business about how it would ruin her if she had to come forward—that don't make sense."

"But here's the thing," Fargo went on. "I'm worried about the rest of the gals at the Sawdust Corner. Seems to me Scully is hell-bent on getting whatever Dora Hightower has in that box. Good chance he'll turn to the others, or Bob Skinner, to find out where Dora is hiding out."

"I take your drift," Vance said. "You're wondering if I'd be willing to spend a lot more time at the saloon."

Fargo nodded. "Seems to me a former Texas Ranger has to be a dead shot. And Bob's got a messenger gun under that bar that would make any man think twice. And he might be ugly as a mud fence, but he's got sand."

"There's one problem: the dime-a-dance gals work in different shifts, and all of them board at Ma Kunkle's. I can't be two places at once."

"Yeah, I been thinking about that, too. You know Ma Kunkle pretty good, right?"

"I don't stay there—I stay here in my office to keep down expenses. But I see her every day. She's a crusty old gal, but we're good friends."

"I was counting on that," Fargo said. "If you're willing to go along with me, I'll need you to talk to her."

A few hours after sundown, two well-armed riders tied off their horses at the snorting post in front of Ma Kunkle's big two-story boardinghouse. Both men carried coils of rope.

As they headed toward the front porch, spurs chinging, one elbowed the other in the side.

"Lookit, Jeb," he said, pointing toward a sign over the front door. A lantern hung on a nail clearly illuminated the sign:

TRESPASSERS WILL BE SHOT AT
AND IF MISSED WILL BE PROSECUTED

"I'm shittin' my pants," Jeb replied in a tone laced with derision. "Scully said she's an ornery old bitch, so we best find her first and tie her down. But don't leave no marks on her or any of the calicos, Lumpy. This town's already stirred up over what happened to the Hightower bunch."

Both men cleared leather and stepped into a small front parlor that smelled of pleasant cooking odors. A few sticks of old furniture, none of it matching, were scattered around. Flames crackled in a small fieldstone fireplace. The parlor was empty except for a silver-haired, bespectacled man with a salt-and-pepper beard. He sat in a chintz-covered chair reading a clasp Bible by the light of a coal-oil lamp. He was dressed in clergy black and wore a cleric's collar.

"Well, ain't this the berries?" Jeb said. "A holy man. Tell you what, preacher: you can dog-ear that Bible all you want to, but it ain't worth one piece of juicy poon."

The elderly preacher nervously pushed his spectacles higher on the bridge of his nose. "Gentlemen, there's no need for those guns. This is a peaceful place."

"Serve it on toast," Lumpy growled. "We're lookin' for a woman—a blond-haired woman so beautiful, she could make a dead man come. Where is she?"

"Gentlemen, I truly do not know whom you speak of. I just arrived in town today and haven't even spent one night under this roof."

Jeb shot a glance at Lumpy, who shook his head. Roughing up a preacher would be just as dangerous as hurting a woman. Lumpy holstered his gun and Jeb followed suit.

"All right," Jeb said. "We ain't here to cause no trouble, preacher. The reason we had our guns out, see, we're lookin' for our sister, and she's being held by a bad hombre who's

137

keeping her a sorta prisoner, you might say. Beats her and such."

"My goodness," the preacher replied. "I do hope you will use no violence if you locate her."

"Never mind the sermon. Where's the old woman—Ma Kunkle? She might be able to help us."

"I believe she's in the kitchen at the end of the hallway. But I hope you won't—"

"Don't worry. We're only here to find our sister."

Libby Snyder opened her door just then to go visit one of the girls in another room. She literally bumped into one of the two unshaven, hard-bitten men as they passed by in the hallway. She started to duck back into her room, but he caught her by the upper arm.

"Say, now!" he exclaimed, eyes undressing the pretty brunette. "What's cookin', good-lookin'? Look what we got here, Lumpy. Lookit the puffy loaves on this little heifer. Ma Kunkle can wait a bit."

They pushed her back inside the room.

"Where's Belle Star's room?" the hard case demanded.

"She doesn't live at this boardinghouse."

Jeb gave her a vicious backhand. "Pitch it to hell, bitch! I asked you where Belle Star's room is, and by God you'd better tell me."

Libby struggled to break free. "I told you she doesn't live here. Last I heard from Bob Skinner, she just up and quit her job and left town."

"So that's how you're gonna play it, huh? Say, Lumpy, we can't tell if the wood is good just by looking at the paint."

With a hard tug he ripped the bodice off her dress. His face twisted into a mask of lust as he stared at the woman's tits. "Oh, hey! We ain't even gonna charge you a stud fee, sugar britches. Kick that door shut, Lumpy. Me and you are gonna—"

The sound of the sudden gunshots seemed incredibly loud inside the room. The back of Jeb's skull exploded, and Lumpy had twisted halfway around when the preacher fired his second shot, the bullet punching into Lumpy's right eye. The preacher fired a third time, this shot blowing a hole into the thug's forehead. He landed atop his dead companion, his bootheels scratching the rose-pattern carpet a few times as his nervous system registered its last reaction.

Sitch McDougall stood rooted, his Remington giving off blue wisps of smoke as his heart stomped against his ribs. Then his knees suddenly turned to water, and he was forced to brace himself with one hand on the doorframe as a paralyzing numbness came over him.

He had never killed a man in his life, and here he had just killed two. The penny dreadfuls never mentioned the sudden stench of feces and urine when a dead man's bowels and bladder released in death, or the oddly metallic odor of copious amounts of fresh blood.

Libby, covered in some of that blood, rushed to his side. "Sit down, Mr. McDougall," she ordered, leading him toward a chair.

He didn't hear her, staring at the lifeless bodies as she pulled him toward the chair. Three quick shots and he had canceled two lives. He had no regrets, but he realized he had just crossed an epic divide. Every time he looked in a mirror to shave from now until the end of his days, the eyes of a killer would be staring back at him.

"Sitch!" Libby said loudly, trying to snap him out of his daze. "You were wonderful! I'm proud of you."

He nodded woodenly but said nothing. He remembered something Fargo had said to him in camp a few nights ago: *Every killing has to mean something to you, has to always bother you a little no matter how justified it is. That's the difference between a killer and a murderer. Taking any human life has to matter.*

Ma Kunkle had been working in the kitchen when the two intruders entered her house. She had finished cooking a slab of beef and had packed it into a tall crock. She was just pouring hot lard over it to preserve it when the shots rang out.

She grabbed the Colt Dragoon lying on the counter and hustled down the hallway toward Libby Snyder's room, where gray-white powder smoke hazed the hallway outside the door.

She peeked cautiously around the door, and then a satisfied smile divided her careworn face. Skye Fargo and the sheriff had been right.

She took in Sitch McDougall's chalk white face. He still clutched the Bible in his left hand. "You didn't kill two men, son. Just two filthy hyenas who are already burning in hell. I'm awful glad you were here."

Sitch finally found his voice. "They were men, all right, Mrs. Kunkle. But just like Fargo puts it: They required killing."

19

About two hours after Sitch McDougall had notched his first kill, Skye Fargo was slowly inching forward on his stomach, getting into better position to hear what was being said around the campfire at Rough and Ready.

But the unexpected news he was about to hear would chill his blood.

He had hobbled the Ovaro about a half mile to the west in a narrow draw and approached on foot until he was about a hundred yards out. He had low-crawled the rest of the way into the camp, a long, slow process occasionally interrupted by a roving sentry.

Iron Mike Scully and his favorite dirt workers, Romer Stanton and Leroy Jackman, had been speaking in low, urgent voices while sharing a bottle of whiskey. And apparently, despite Fargo's efforts and Otis Mumford's exposure of the "haunted valley" hoax, he had been too late. So far as Fargo could tell, every miner not riding for the red sashes had pulled up stakes. The cluster of tents was gone, and the little clapboard shanties appeared deserted.

Scully had pulled that part off somehow, Fargo realized. But it had gotten the greedy murderer nothing—without that map or whatever Dora Hightower was safeguarding, the sashes were dining on air pudding. And Fargo had come here tonight because there was one essential fact he still needed to know.

Fargo, pressed flat behind a dead log, heard a rider approaching at a canter. He reined in near the fire and dismounted.

"What's the word, Dakota?" Scully called out. "Any luck?"

"Luck? Mike, we're screwed, glued and tattooed."

"Well, don't just stand there like a schoolgirl with a secret," Scully snapped. "Give."

"Lumpy and Jeb went to the boardinghouse, just like you ordered. And now they're both cold as a basement floor."

"Christ! Fargo did it?"

"Now, that's the queer part of it," Dakota replied as more red sashes materialized out of the surrounding darkness to hear the news. "It was a goddamn preacher who laid them out—some little nancy with silver hair and spectacles."

Fargo was stunned at the news. His faith in Sitch McDougall had been justified after all.

"A preach—?"

Scully suddenly fell silent. Fargo, only ten yards away, watched his cruel, thin-lipped mouth twist with rage.

"Boys, that wasn't no damn preacher. 'Member all them disguise doodads the whip boy had in his saddlebag—the fake beards and such? There was specs and a holy man's collar in that bag, too. Son of a *bitch*!"

Scully threw the empty whiskey bottle hard into a tree. "What about the saloon?"

"No soap," Dakota replied. "That damn weak-bellied sheriff has roosted there, bold as a big man's ass. And Bob Skinner has got that double-ten right out in plain view. We couldn't lay a hand on any of the gals."

"Boss, I don't like this shit," Leroy Jackman said in his hillman's twang. "If we don't—"

"Stow it," Scully snarled. "What *you* like ain't nothing to the matter. I'm the rainmaker around here."

"Well, you ain't making much damn rain, Iron Mike," called out a voice from just beyond the circle of firelight. "This Trailsman is everything he's cracked up to be. Already him and that pasty-face sidekick of his has killed six of us and busted up two more—busted 'em up bad."

"Where do you get six killed?" Scully challenged belligerently. "I make it five."

"Tim Ulrick just died—he's the one that was wounded in the hay wagon."

Scully cursed. "All right, boys, I'll admit that Fargo is about half rough. But you got to see this thing right. Romer's little trick with the cow bladder sent the last of the miners skedaddling. We *own* this place now. Either Fargo or the Hightower bitch has that map, and once we lay hands on it, there's no more hog and hominy on *our* plates. We don't share no profits with nobody. We can bring a bunch of coolies in here to mine that silver for fifty cents a day. Or if the price is right, we'll just sell that paper to one of the big outfits."

"Once we lay hands on that map, huh?" Dakota said. "And what if Fargo's got it? First we'd have to track down the bastard and then we have to kill him. I'd rather share a small barrel with a big badger."

A few voices chorused assent.

"Reach down in your pants," Scully said scornfully, "and see if you own a pair. You boys know who I am, and you know my reputation as a gunny. Romer and Leroy here are some pumpkins with a long gun, and plenty of you boys ain't no slouches, neither. Never mind the goddamn 'legend' of Skye Fargo. He's just a man who bleeds like all the rest."

"Yeah, 'cept *we* been doing all the bleeding." Another voice spoke up. "Mike, it was you three that killed that family and now you've brought down the wrath on all of us."

"Boys, we *had* to kill Clement Hightower. The son of a bitch wanted half the profits. And how could we snuff his wick and leave his family as witnesses?"

"Half of something is better'n all of nothing. You went too damn far when you done that, and I'm clearing out before Fargo plants me, too."

"So am I," Dakota said. "Any of you boys who are with me, I'm leaving at first light."

Fargo's lips pressed into a grim, determined slit. This was the key fact that had been missing. He suspected all along that Scully, Romer and Leroy had done the killing on their own, but he wanted confirmation none of the others was involved before he closed out their accounts permanently.

"Listen, you chicken guts," Scully said, rising to his feet. "Don't be fools. The bunch of us has been riding together since we split off from the Pukes in Missouri. Have I ever fouled our nest even once?"

"No," Dakota admitted. "You been a good leader, Iron

Mike. I've had more shiners in my pockets, since I took up with you, than I ever seen in my life. You're the toughest hombre I ever rode with. But this time it's different—this time you got Skye Fargo riled when you three slaughtered women and kids. And he ain't gonna let go of this, Mike. He's like a bulldog on a pant leg, and he *ain't* gonna let it go."

"He will when I kill him."

"I wish you luck there, I truly do. If any man can do it, it's you. But I'm puttin' this place far behind me."

Scully spat into the fire. "All right, Dakota, I ain't your mother. How many of you boys are sticking besides Romer and Leroy?"

Not one voice spoke up. Only the low moaning of the nighttime wind broke up a silence that was deafening.

"All right, then," Scully said. "But don't come crawling back when you hear that us three are rolling in it. You had your chance."

The men dispersed, heading for their bedrolls. When no one was within hearing, Romer Stanton's ferret face suddenly went jubilant. "By God, Mike, you oughter be on stage in Frisco. It went just like you said it would."

This sudden, unexpected turn in the trail struck Fargo as both surprising and ominous.

"Like I told you boys," Scully said, "a pie split three ways looks better than a pie split ten ways. But let's just hush down for now. There's a good chance Fargo is listening to us right now."

Romer's jubilation transformed into nervousness as he glanced around at the surrounding shadows. "How you mean, boss?"

"Think about it, boyo. When Otis Mumford put out that story of his, I just figured Fargo had sniffed out the clearing and found our gear. But then I started puzzling on it. It just ain't too likely he'd a thought to search the trees overhead, now is it?"

"*Hell* no," Leroy said, catching on. "The magic lantern . . . that was in the story. But we had it hid way up in a tree. Which means Fargo spied on us while we was there."

"Shit," Romer said, suddenly scootching back from the

firelight. "Happens he's out there, he could kill all of us right now."

"He won't," Scully assured him. "He has to be too far from his horse and there's too many men here to risk it. But just to play it safe—"

Scully quickly kicked dirt over the fire, plunging the camp into darkness. "Hey, Fargo!" he called out, his voice smug with triumph. "Is the great *legend* out there? If you are, I got a suggestion: why'n't you ride back to Peatross's livery and see if your sweet little gal is still hiding in the hay?"

Scully's last remark struck Fargo with the force of hard slaps. He had no choice but to retreat slowly and with infinite care. He had shoehorned himself into a good listening post never expecting that it would matter how long it took him to get back out. But now every second weighed on him with the urgency of a death sentence—Dora Hightower's death sentence.

How, he wondered repeatedly, could Scully have found out that Dora was hidden in the livery? It seemed like the last place the sashes would have searched for her, which was why Fargo had picked the place. Despite all the caution he had taken to get her there unobserved, maybe there had been another one of Scully's spies watching.

When he had finally crawled far enough away from the camp, he sprinted the half mile back to his stallion.

He had already instructed Sitch to stay at the boardinghouse until Fargo returned to town. He found him—minus the preacher disguise—asleep in a chair in Libby's room.

"You should've seen it, Fargo," Sitch boasted as Fargo hustled him toward the front door. "I—"

"I'm damn proud of you," Fargo cut him off, "but right now we got bigger fish to fry. Hop your horse. Scully found out that Dora is hiding in the livery."

"Jesus! Has he— I mean, is she—?"

"Damned if I know anything more," Fargo said as he stepped up and over and reined the Ovaro around.

Both men shucked out their short irons as they rode into the hoof-packed yard, but no ambush awaited them. They found Peatross in the tack room, bound and gagged and with a bloody gash over his right eye. Fargo removed the gag and started untying the ropes.

"The hell happened here, old-timer?" Fargo demanded.

"All hell was a-poppin', Fargo. Two hard cases come in just as I was settling into sleep. I recognized 'em right off as two of Scully's men. One carried a Sharps fifty, the other an old Hawken."

"Romer and Leroy," Fargo said grimly. "Then what?"

"One of 'em conked me on the cabeza with the butt of his short gun. It didn't quite knock me out, but I let on like it did. They gagged me and tied me up. They sneaked up in the loft and caught the gal asleep. I barely heard a peep outta her before they gagged her, too. They was up there a few minutes rummaging around, then left with her."

"At least they didn't kill her—right off, anyway," Fargo muttered to Sitch. "But I wonder if they got what Scully's been after. If they did, she's likely dead by now."

Peatross, walking unsteadily like a sailor with sea legs, crossed to a bench. "If you mean this, they ain't got it."

He spilled out the contents of a coffee can filled with horseshoe nails. The felt-covered box tumbled out from the bottom. "She asked me to hide it real good for her."

"Good," Fargo said in a tone of relief. "They won't kill her until they lay hands on that."

Fargo opened the box and removed a sheet of onionskin paper, carefully unfolding it. It seemed to be a combination of map and technical diagram.

"I peeked at it," Peatross confessed. "Couldn't make hide nor hair out of it, though."

"Me either," Fargo said, "but a man experienced in mining could."

"Anyhow," Peatross said, "I don't think they believed she had it. I heard them two snake shits slapping her around up in the loft, asking her over and over if you had it."

"And now I *do* have it. They'll keep her alive as a bargaining chip to get it from me. When did they get here?"

"It was mebbe an hour or two after dark—I turn in early."

Fargo expelled a weary sigh. "Damn it! I underrated Scully—a stupid mistake on my part. That means he, Romer and Leroy already knew she was here before he sent the rest of his curs to the boardinghouse and the saloon. It was brilliant—he kept everything secret even from most of his men. A classic feint. We were watching all the wrong places when the attack came."

"Yeah," Sitch pitched in, "but how did they know Dora was here?"

"Dora?" Peatross repeated, confused. "I thought her name was Belle?"

"Never mind. It's a long story," Fargo said impatiently.

"Anyhow," Peatross said, his grizzled face looking chagrined, "there ain't no mystery about how they knew she was here. Fargo, you might say we saw everything 'cept the three waltzing elephants. Neither one of us remembered about Walt— that freckle-faced kid who comes here a few hours a day to shovel manure and such."

"You mean you let him see her?"

"I didn't *let* him do nothing." The old hostler bristled. "Earlier today I had to leave for a couple hours to help a rancher south of here with a mare that was foaling. I forgot the kid was coming in to clean out stalls. He had to go into the loft to fork down some hay, and he musta seen her and talked it around town enough that one of Scully's men heard about it."

"Hell, Methuselah," Sitch complained, "seems like you would've remembered and—"

"Shit, piss and corruption!" Peatross fumed. "Did either of you two think about it? I'll tan that sprout's britches when I see him."

"Never mind," Fargo said, pouring oil on the waters. "It doesn't matter now, and who can blame the kid? Hell, he sees an angel living in a hayloft and doesn't know thing one about what's happening. Naturally he'd spread it around. The thing now is to get Dora back in one piece."

"They could've taken her anywhere," Sitch said.

Fargo thought about that and then shook his head. "Not right off they didn't—or at least they didn't take her anywhere too far away. Romer and Leroy were both back in camp when I got there."

"You think they took her back to Rough and Ready?"

Fargo nodded. "Bound and gagged her and hid her where the rest couldn't see her. Hell, I might've been ten feet away from her in the dark and didn't know it."

"Maybe we could ride back right now—"

"Nix on that. Scully guessed that I might be spying on them, and he deliberately sent me back here so I could find out they had her. That tells me they plan to move her somewhere—maybe they already have. But even if they've still got her at their camp, it's a fool's errand to try rescuing her tonight. Scully's men have dumped the blanket and they're riding out in the morning. But until they're gone, that still leaves too many guns for us to take on."

"So we go after her tomorrow?"

"We'll bed down here for the night and ride out there at first light," Fargo said. "But there's only three of them left now, and that camp's a lousy defensive position in daylight. They'll likely move her to a better spot. They know I'm a tracker and they'll be sure to leave a clear trail. The girl is useless to them without me. I've got what they want."

"A gal that peart," Peatross put in, "ain't 'useless' to a bunch of horny sage rats. They're likely taking turns on her right now."

"You're a sunshine peddler, all right," Fargo said sarcastically. "There's nothing we can do about that. Things are the way they are, and we need to worry about getting her back alive."

"They won't trade her even up for that map," Sitch said. "They *can't* leave her alive. Nor us. We'll be riding into some kind of trap where they plan to kill all three of us."

"Of course," Fargo replied. "Like I just said: things are the way they are."

20

The new day's sun was still a blush on the eastern horizon when Fargo and Sitch McDougall rode north from Carson City, headed toward the mining camp.

"Rough and Ready," Sitch remarked, breath ghosting in the chill autumn air. "I guess we'd better be."

"Never mind the quaint observations," Fargo said. "Keep your eyes to all sides for an ambush. Remember, they won't parley with us if they can avoid it. It's not carved in stone that they'll hustle Dora off to some new hidey-hole. They could try to wipe us out of our saddles at any moment."

"Wouldn't that be risky for them? I mean, what if you stashed that map someplace? If they kill you, there goes their bonanza in silver."

Fargo, whose eyes scanned the terrain with the relentless attention of a veteran frontier scout, shook his head.

"They'll assume the map is with me," he said with assurance. "They figure I can't get Dora without it."

"*Is* it with you?"

Fargo nodded. "I don't know how things are going to shake out, so I had to bring it. You just remember: They'll do their damnedest to kill us at long range. And there's no better weapons for that than a Sharps fifty or a Hawken gun, both of which they have."

The two horsebackers held their mounts at a lope, a good pace that a horse could hold without quickly tiring, yet one fast enough to make the riders difficult targets. Fargo was more concerned about the trio of murderers killing the horses, far easier targets. Forcing a man to shank's mare in this territory was a sure and certain death sentence if shooters were determined to kill him.

Fargo hauled back on the reins about two hundred yards from the camp. They hobbled their mounts in a deep erosion gully and approached the camp on foot as the sun began to heat the air.

"Looks deserted," Fargo said as the two men studied the place from behind a deadfall of tangled branches. "No horses in sight. Let's see if we can pick up a trail."

Holding his Henry at the ready, Fargo cautiously led the way forward, his eyes in constant motion. The silence of the apparently deserted camp seemed eerie and somehow ominous. Danger sometimes left a certain texture in the air, and Fargo felt it now: a slightly charged quality that he felt right before a huge bolt of lightning struck.

Fargo began "mouse-trapping" the deserted structures, cautiously approaching the entrances from one side to make sure they were clear. He was only about ten feet away from a dilapidated shack when the back of his neck began to prickle.

Simultaneously, the insect hum suddenly fell silent.

"Kiss the dirt!" he shouted to Sitch, leaping back and falling flat on the ground face-first. An explosion rocked the ground and sent dirt and debris hurtling into the air, showering both men. Moments later Fargo heard the rataplan of escaping hooves.

"What the *hell*?" Sitch managed when he got his wits about him and cautiously sat up.

"Crater charge," Fargo explained, rising to his knees. "Don't forget, we're in a mining camp."

"Yeah, but how'd they set it off without us seeing them do it?"

"Galvanic detonator," Fargo explained. "They were just invented. You push down a plunger and a galvanic current travels along a wire to a percussion cap on the charge."

"It was inside that shack we were about to check out," Sitch said. "A few feet more and we'd both be playing harps. How'd you know?"

"I didn't exactly *know*. But when you hear the insects suddenly go quiet, it's best to harken and heed. Well, whoever almost blew us to smithereens rode out to the northwest. We should have a fresh trail."

They found the detonator in a clump of juniper on the

northern edge of the camp. Fargo tucked at the knees to read the sign.

"Fresh prints are moister than old ones. Two riders rode out well before dawn, judging from the crumbling at the edge of the prints as they've started to dry," he remarked to Sitch. "The dirt is still fresh in the third set of prints. They all head in the same direction, so whoever tried to kill us just now is going to join the other two."

"I wonder how far away they are," Sitch said as the two men hoofed it back to their hidden mounts.

"I'd say close by," Fargo surmised. "They aren't running from us, they're luring us into a trap. Most likely they'll pick the first place they think is a good defensive position."

"And try to pick us off from ambush as we close in?"

"That'll be a mite harder to do now because the terrain is thinning out to desert hills. And we've got all three sets of prints to go by. If they try to ambush us from a flank, we'll see human or horse prints veering off. The big idea now is for us to try to guess where their nest is before we ride into range of those long guns."

They retrieved their mounts and picked up the trail, Fargo dividing his attention between the tracks close at hand and the terrain out ahead, using his field glasses constantly to read the geography. For several miles there wasn't much to worry about—all three sets of prints showed no veering to the flanks, and the terrain features offered no good places to fort up.

Eventually, however, they topped a low rise and Fargo reined in, making a long study through the glasses.

"I got a hunch we might be hugging with them soon," he remarked. "Take a look."

Sitch peered into the glasses. Well out ahead, still out of rifle range, was a cluster of granite boulders atop a steep ridge. The location left an excellent view to all sides.

"Well, if they're up there," he said, "how do we get at them? Even I know you always want the high ground in a fight."

Fargo nodded. "Sure. But there ain't no horse that can't be rode, and there ain't no man that can't be throwed."

Sitch's brow furrowed in puzzlement. "Meaning . . . ?"

"Meaning when you can't blast your way in a-smokin', you switch to wit and wile. First of all—"

Fargo reached across and snatched the garish hat off his companion's head. "Hats are easy to spot against the color of this sand—and this conk cover you've got on could be spotted from New Orleans."

Fargo swung down and removed his own hat. "I hope Scully hasn't got spyglasses. If not, they shouldn't be able to see us yet. Light down and hobble that sorrel. We're leaving our mounts right here."

Fargo slid his Henry from its boot. "That old harmonica pistol of yours—is it charged and loaded?"

"All ten barrels. I can't be sure the powder hasn't clumped by now, though."

"I've got a flask of black powder. Reload all ten barrels. You'll be needing them."

"Fargo, I can hit a bull in the butt with a banjo, maybe, but this harmonica—"

"Don't worry. You won't need to hit anything. You're going to be a diversion. You're going to head due west from here, staying far enough that you're out of rifle range. Then you're going to head north again until you're on a straight bead with that boulder cluster. Head back east toward them, but stay low and *don't* get close enough that they can shoot you."

"But won't they spot me?"

"That's all right if they do because I'll make sure they don't spot me. I want them to think that we're together and that I'm just better at hiding than you are. I'll be approaching from the east, out of the sun, and I'll be low-crawling."

Sitch paled as something occurred to him. "What if they just ride out and kill me?"

"They won't. They'll be scared that maybe that's our plan and that I'm hidden somewhere waiting to plug them with my Henry. Now listen—you've got to be close enough that they at least hear your weapons. I want you to fire off some rounds from the harmonica, then from the Remington, and keep switching back and forth. I want them to hear two weapons. Does that watch of yours work?"

"Sure. I only steal the best."

152

Sitch pulled a gold-cased watch from his fob pocket. "Right now it's—"

"Don't tell me." Fargo glanced toward the sun, shading his eyes and calculating its distance from the horizon. "It's nearbout ten o'clock, right?"

Sitch's eyes widened. "Say! It's only five minutes after. You're pretty good."

"I'd better be," Fargo said grimly, "because accurate timing is what this deal is all about now."

Fargo did some quick calculating. If he botched this part of it, the whole shebang would come down and bury both of them in the rubble of lousy planning.

"All right," he finally said. "We should both be in place by eleven thirty. That's when I want you to open up. But listen—dig a little sand wallow first just in case you miscalculate the distance. Keep your damn head down, hear?"

"I hear, but aren't you forgetting something? We haven't seen any sign at all that anybody is hiding among those boulders. What if we go through all this shit and they're someplace else?"

"You pay your money," Fargo replied, "and you take your chances. I'm rolling the dice and hoping they come up seven. Remember, I make the medicine—"

"And I take it," Sitch finished for him. Then he paled even more until his face looked fish-belly white. "But, hold on—what if they kill you?"

Fargo grinned wickedly. "Then we'll *both* soon be worm castles. What the hell—when you were stupid enough to come west, did you expect to live forever?"

"Well, at least make sure you kill Iron Mike first. He can draw that side iron of his faster than eyesight."

Fargo shook his head. For a painful moment the awful tableau was again etched clearly in his mind: women and children lying dead in the Nevada sand. And it was Iron Mike Scully who gave the order and led the killing. Now Fargo intended to buck Scully out in smoke even if the Trailsman had to die trying.

"You got it bass-ackwards, old son. Iron Mike and me will be hugging last. Now shut your fish trap and get going, and for Christsakes, stay as low as you can get. Remember, start cracking caps at eleven thirty sharp."

"But—"

"But me no buts," Fargo cut him off. "If a man out west starts worrying about all the ways he might die, he'll never get out of bed. Now put some stiff in your spine and get moving."

21

Fargo hooked to the east, counting on his buckskins to blend well with the dark sand. By now the sun was heating up with a vengeance, and sweat rolled freely out of his hairline, evaporating almost instantly in the dry desert air.

He turned due north, advancing in a crouch and keeping the nest of boulders well to his left. At the top of the ridge he advanced west as far as he dared on foot and then dropped to the ground for a long, grueling crawl. Now and then he glanced at the sun to judge the time.

From long experience in cover and concealment Fargo had learned that no ground was ever truly flat. Now and then he stopped and laid one side of his head down in the sand, studying the ridgeline from ground level. With careful and constant observation, a man could spot little depressions and folds to keep him at least partially below the skyline.

The hot, broiling sun behind him was his best ally right now. Anyone looking in this direction—and he was certain the three butchers were watching in every direction—would be greatly impeded. Relentlessly he inched forward, at times forced to squirm like a snake in loose sand. His progress was made even more awkward because the brass frame of his rifle forced him to keep the weapon tucked under his side to cut telltale reflection.

So far he had spotted no one within the boulders and wondered if Sitch had been right after all—maybe they weren't even there. But there was no help for it. A man had to play the hand he was dealt, and his only choice was to play those cards as best he could.

He tried not to think too much about Dora. He assumed she was still alive since Scully needed her as a bargaining chip. But given the low-life predators who had abducted her, a woman might very well prefer death to whatever they might be doing to her.

Fargo glanced up at the shimmering sun. It would soon be time for Sitch to open fire, and now the Trailsman realized he should have allowed more time. It was up to the Henry and his aim to pull this off, and after his first shot he had to get back on bead and fire a second one with incredible speed.

When Sitch opened fire about fifteen minutes later, the shots sounded like insignificant little popping sounds. But they were enough to confirm Fargo's hunch: three heads appeared over the boulders to search toward the west. Scully was easy to identify from the long hair tied into a knot on his nape.

Fargo reacted with the machine reflexes of a man for whom life had often depended on speed, precision and cool nerves.

BRASS, he reminded himself, the only system that allowed a man to score head shots at this distance.

Breathe. He took in a deep breath and expelled it slowly and evenly as he carried out the rest.

Relax. He willed his muscles to go heavy as the tension left them.

Aim. He dropped the Henry's notch sight on the head of one of the men holding a rifle—Romer Stanton.

Slack and *squeeze.* With a steady, even pressure he eased his trigger finger back until the slack gave way to the pressure of the sear. A heartbeat later the Henry bucked into his shoulder and Fargo watched an explosion of blood as his round destroyed Stanton's head.

But he immediately worked the Henry's lever and notched his sight on Leroy Jackman, realizing there was no time for finesse with this shot. Fargo's first shot missed, but the second punched into Jackman's skull and he dropped like a sack of grain.

That took care of the rifle marksmen, Fargo realized. But Iron Mike Scully had ducked down by now—exactly as Fargo had hoped he would.

When he came back up into view, he held Dora Hightower

in front of him. Her mouth was gagged and her hands tied behind her.

"Good shooting, Fargo!" he roared out. "But I still got the bitch! So how you wanna play it?"

Fargo stood up in plain view, knowing that even a pistolero like Scully couldn't kill with a short iron at this distance.

"Like this," Fargo shouted back. "I'll toss my Henry and you'll toss those two long guns out where I can see 'em. Then we'll play to your strength—a shootout with our sidearms."

"You're calling *me* out for a showdown with six-guns? What, you think I'm some Iowa hayseed? You wouldn't be that stupid. What's your grift?"

"No grift. What you see is what you get. Think about it—all three of you cockroaches were exposed when I opened fire. If I wanted to kill you first, I'd've done it right then. But with you, I want it face to face."

"All right, asshole, it's your funeral."

Scully tossed both of the rifles out and emerged from the nest of boulders, still keeping Dora in front of him.

Fargo slowly reached into his possibles bag and produced a little chamois pouch weighted down with a stone. "Here's something to make it interesting. Catch."

Fargo flipped the pouch toward Scully, who caught it with his left hand. He opened the drawstring with his teeth and peered inside.

"A poker chip? What, you getting cute on me, long shanks?"

"Nope. I know how much you like the poker-chip draw. I've got a chip, too. We'll both put a chip on the back of our hands and extend them straight out from our side. We'll see who can kill who before the chips hit the ground."

"Fargo, you showboating asshole! You seen what I did at the Sawdust Corner."

"That's true," Fargo said. "But you didn't see what I can do, did you? And this time you won't be shooting into a saloon floor."

For a moment the smug confidence on Scully's face wavered, the cruel, thin-lipped smile almost fading. But only for a moment.

"Shit, crusader, you're just running a bluff."

"Opinions vary," Fargo said calmly. "Now, let's cut the hot-jawing. Push that girl aside and let's get thrashing."

In fact Fargo *was* bluffing. He knew damn well that Scully was a faster draw than he was. Unlike criminal trash like him, Fargo didn't spend hours in front of hotel mirrors practicing.

But he also knew that plenty of "trick shots" like Scully, ruthless murderers of women and children, were cowards at heart and could be goaded to buck fever in an actual draw-shoot. In their nervous excitement they tended to fire too quickly after jerking their guns out, and the slightest buck-ing of a six-shooter would throw it off bead. That was why Fargo was staying twenty yards back. At this distance, any miscalculation with a six-gun would prove critical. Fargo knew it was the first man to score a hit who would win, not the first to clear leather.

"Move in a little closer," Scully ordered.

"S'matter, big man?" Fargo taunted. "The distance is the same for both of us."

"Eat shit, buckskins!"

Scully roughly pushed Dora to one side. Each man placed his poker chip on the back of his gunhand and extended his arm straight out to his side. Fargo noticed a slight tremble in Scully's hand. But his voice was strong and confident:

"Make your play, hero."

Fargo waited for perhaps ten seconds, a little smile on his face as his implacable eyes bored into Scully's.

"Jerk it back, cockchafer!" Scully snarled. "If you got the balls to do it."

Fargo flipped his hand and cleared leather in a blur of speed before his chip hit the ground. But as he had expected, Scully was faster. His gun barked and Fargo felt a sharp tug at the left side of his shirt, the bullet creasing his side like a red-hot wire. Fargo's shot came a half second later, and he didn't risk trying for a head shot. His bullet punched into Scully just below the breastbone, and he staggered to one side screaming with pain as he went down.

Iron Mike's smoking gun was still in his hand, and Fargo took no chances. He pumped three more slugs into his adversary, and suddenly it was over like a curtain dropping at the end of a play.

Powder smoke hazed the air around Fargo along with the sulfurous stench of spent gunpowder. Dora, whose nerves had been stretched tight on tenterhooks since her abduction the night before, fainted dead away. Even Fargo, now that it was over, had to drop to one knee as the strength momentarily drained from his legs.

Nothing, Fargo realized, would bring the Hightower family back from their graves—graves he had dug. He felt no great satisfaction in killing these three curs. Like he had told Sitch a few nights back: taking any human life has to matter.

But maybe, just maybe, he had saved the next family, and that was a good enough day's work for Skye Fargo.

22

"Here's a corker," Sitch told the men around him at the bar. "There's this railroad baron, see, and he travels from Chicago to Saint Louis for a big meeting. But the hotel where the meeting is being held burns down just before he gets there and the meeting is canceled. So he sends a telegram to his wife telling her he'll be coming home early.

"Well, he gets home and unlocks the door, and there's his wife getting the hell screwed out of her by the butler. He storms out and goes to live in a hotel. The next day his mother-in-law shows up all smiles. 'James,' she says, 'pack up your things and go home. I talked to Carrie and it's all just a big misunderstanding. You see, she never got your telegram!'"

Fargo's lips twitched in a weak grin, Sheriff Vance shook his head in disgust, and Bob Skinner looked bored.

"You're actually hiring on this horse thief, Bob?" the sheriff asked.

"Yeah, but not for his damn stale jokes. He cracks a mean whip, Cyrus. He'll draw in more customers than the upstairs gals do."

"Yeah, 'specially now that he's a big grizz-bear killer," the sheriff added in a tone laced with sarcasm, eyeing the claw necklace Sitch had removed from Iron Mike Scully's corpse. "And you'd *better* send that sorrel back up to its rightful owner," he added.

"It's the right thing to do," Sitch replied solemnly, "especially for a preacher like me," and Bob Skinner snorted.

"Where you headed, Fargo?" the sheriff asked, grimacing as he forced down a belt of warm milk.

"First I'm riding to Fort Churchill to square with the

army. Colonel Mackenzie will likely cashier me, but I was going to quit anyhow. He'll at least pay my back wages after he reads me the riot act."

"Well, you'll face no legal problems," Vance assured him. "Everybody knows the miners pulled foot, and by now the buzzards are picking those three sashes apart out in the desert. Nobody even knows you sent them under. You seen that new broadsheet from the *Territorial Enterprise* up on the Comstock. They backed way off that story about you and whip boy here wiping out the Hightower family. It would still be better, though, if Dora would come forward and tell Otis Mumford what really happened."

Fargo nodded and looked at the barkeep. "So she decided to stay on a while?"

"Yep. She'll be singing and dancing and staying in the room at the back just like before. She's sorta at loose ends right now. She needs to figure out what she's going to do with that map."

"I've got some ideas in that direction," Fargo said.

"I sure wish I knew what she's holding back," the sheriff said. "When I told her it was safe to go to Otis now and spill her story about the sashes, she turned white on me. If she—"

The door in the side wall opened and Dora Hightower emerged wearing a flower-print dress. She flashed all the men a pearly smile.

"Sheriff, Skye, Mitt, would you three gentlemen please join me at a table? I'd like to speak with you."

She led Fargo and the others to a table near the rear of the nearly empty Sawdust Corner.

"First of all," she said, sharing a glance between Fargo and Sitch, "I can't tell you two how grateful I am for everything you did to help me. Nothing will bring my family back, but at least I know that their killers received justice. And thanks to your efforts, the silver my brother worked so hard to locate won't end up profiting murderers. Both of you are heroes."

"A Sitch in time saves the mine," Sitch quipped, and the sheriff frowned.

"You'd've rooked her out of that silver if you had half a chance," he said. "And take that damn foolish hat off before I shoot you."

"About that silver," Fargo said to Dora, "have you made any plans?"

She shook her head. "I'm helpless when it comes to such matters. If you have any suggestions . . ."

"I do," Fargo said. "If it hadn't been for the courage of one of the miners at Rough and Ready, a fellow named Duffy Beckman, Sitch and me would be dead and you might be, too. Duffy isn't exactly a mining engineer, but he's got a brother up on the Comstock who is. Duffy is hardworking, good at handling men, and as honest as the day is long. You couldn't get a better man to supervise a mining operation."

"That sounds wonderful, but do you know where he is?"

Fargo nodded. "He's prospecting out at Hat Creek in Modoc County up in the California Sierra. I could have him back here in less than ten days."

"With your recommendation, Skye, I'd be honored to have his assistance."

Dora turned those big, fetching blue eyes on Cyrus Vance. "Sheriff, I've been thinking about what you said, and you're right. I've decided to go see Otis Mumford today and tell him about the attack on my family and identify the attackers. Even though nobody could possibly believe that horrible newspaper story in the *Territorial Enterprise*, I just *must* officially clear Skye and Mitt's names. I just hope . . . that is, I . . ." She trailed off, her pretty face a study in abject misery.

"Listen, Dora," the sheriff coaxed, "if you're in some kind of trouble, you need to tell us. Something is gnawing at you. We're all your friends and you can trust us."

"I'm a fugitive from the law," she blurted out, barely fighting back tears. "A warrant has been issued for my arrest back in Monroe County, Michigan."

Fargo and the sheriff exchanged startled glances. They hadn't expected anything like this.

"Don't stop now," Fargo urged her.

"I'm originally from Valdosta, Georgia. One summer a young gentleman from Michigan came down to visit his married sister, who was our neighbor. He was in the timber business and quite well to do. As they say, it was love at first sight for both of us. We were married and I moved up north with him. My full name is Dora Hightower Gage."

She took a deep breath to steel herself. "Well, his business was thriving until the Panic of 'Fifty-seven came along and ruined it practically overnight. Albert, my husband, was industrious, but he was college educated and unused to manual labor, which was all he could find after that. He lost several menial jobs and we were desperate, losing our home, and unfortunately Al fell in with some bad company."

Her voice rose an octave as the pain of the memory took its toll on her emotions.

"Somehow they convinced him to assist in a bank robbery in the city of Monroe. His only job was to keep watch outside the front doors. But these men were amateurs and they panicked when a clerk pulled out a gun. One of them killed the clerk. They all escaped, and Al hid out at home for several weeks before he was arrested. He's now serving ten years in prison."

"All right," Fargo said, "there it is. But how are *you* a fugitive?"

"The prosecutor in Monroe was new to the job and one of these law-and-order stump screamers. He decided to indict me for harboring a fugitive. I was warned by a lawyer who knew him, and I fled out west to avoid the shame of a public trial. That's how I ended up with my brother's family."

"Harboring a fugitive?" Sheriff Vance repeated. "Your own *husband*? They sure got some queer ideas back in the States. Well, lady, you don't know the West too good. There ain't a state or territory out here that would honor extradition on such a trumped up charge against a female. No woman out here is required or expected to turn her man in for anything, including murder."

"Besides," Fargo added, "even if you'd stayed in Michigan it would likely have been tossed out before it came to trial."

"That's the straight," Sheriff Vance chimed in. "It's called nolle prossed, refusal to prosecute. Happens all the time. You did nothing wrong—just honored your wedding vows. You've built a pimple into a peak in your mind, Dora, that's all."

"Are . . . are you really sure of that, Sheriff Vance?"

"Sure as the Lord made Moses."

Dora's face was suddenly suffused with a combination of joy and relief. Big crystal teardrops rolled out of her eyes, and Dora abruptly dashed back to her room.

"Now what's biting at her?" Sitch wondered.

"Nothing, you knothead," Fargo replied, unfolding from his chair. "Haven't you ever seen a happy woman? Well, boys, I'm off to rile the army and then fetch Duffy. I'll look you both up when I get back."

"Say, Fargo," Sitch spoke up, "did you hear the one about the fat lady and the bearded midget?"

Fargo waved this off. "Save it until I get back."

Fargo strolled off, but only ten seconds after he left, the batwings swung open and he returned, aiming for the table with a resigned look on his face.

"All right, horse thief," he said in a tone of surrender, "tell me about the fat lady and the bearded midget."

LOOKING FORWARD!
The following is the opening
section of the next novel in the exciting
Trailsman series from Signet:

TRAILSMAN #387
APACHE VENDETTA

*1861, New Mexico Territory—no one stops an
Apache out for vengeance.*

Skye Fargo was being shadowed. To have that happen in Black-
foot or Sioux country would be bad. But now he was in Apache
territory, and that was worse. No other tribe could hold a candle
to the Apaches when it came to a silent stalk and kill.

Fargo wasn't there by choice. Colonel Hastings at Fort
Union had sent for him, saying it was urgent he get there as
quickly as possible.

So here Fargo was, pushing his Ovaro hard over the rugged Southwest terrain in the height of summer. The heat was
blistering.

Fargo was a big man, with eyes as blue as a high country
lake and as piercing as a hawk's. Broad of shoulder and
packed with muscle, he wore buckskins and a red bandanna
and a Colt high on his hip.

Fort Union was situated on the Santa Fe Trail, on the west
side of a valley watered by a creek. It was built to protect
travelers from hostiles, particularly the Jicarilla Apaches,

who keenly resented the white invasion of their land and took great delight in ending the life of any white they caught.

And now at least three of them were stalking him.

Fargo had caught on to them by a fluke when he'd stopped to rest at a spring and climbed some boulders to scout the lay of the land ahead. For the briefest instant he'd glimpsed a trio of swarthy forms and then they had melted away. It was a rare mistake on their part.

They were on foot but that hardly mattered. Apaches could run all day and be fresh to run again the next morning. He might outdistance them by riding the stallion into the ground but then they would catch up and he'd be no better off.

So Fargo was being careful not to let the heat take too much of a toll. His eyes under his hat brim were always in motion, flicking right and left and up and ahead, and he often gave quick glances back.

The Apaches hadn't made the same mistake twice. They rarely did. But they were still there, still stalking him. He knew it as surely as he'd ever known anything.

Fargo had tangled with Apaches before. They were some of the most formidable warriors alive and devious as hell. Masters in the art of dispensing death, they had tricks up their sleeves that no one had ever heard of.

Extra cause for Fargo to be extra alert. It was a strain and kept his nerves on edge. Any sound, however slight, caused him to stiffen.

By his reckoning he was a day out of the fort. The sun was about to set, and although he'd like to push on, the Ovaro was lathered with sweat and needed rest. So against his better judgment he sought a spot to stop for the night.

The mountains were as dry as a desert and as wild as the warriors they bred, a hard land with a lot of rock and sparse vegetation.

Fargo had been through this area before and knew of a tank midway along a ridge. Massive boulders hid it. Once among them, he was in welcome shade. The smell of the water brought the Ovaro's head up and made him lick his dry lips in anticipation. But he didn't dare relax. The Apaches were bound to know of the tank, too.

Under the sprawl of giant monoliths, the pool gleamed dusky in the twilight.

Fargo dismounted and stretched and let the stallion dip its muzzle. His hand on his Colt, he studied the soft earth at the tank's edge. Deer had been there and a bobcat. There wasn't a single moccasin print but that didn't mean a thing. Apaches never left tracks if they could help it.

Fargo debated whether to strip his saddle and decided not to. He might need to light a shuck in a hurry. Sliding his Henry rifle from the scabbard, he worked the lever to feed a cartridge into the chamber and sat cross-legged with his back to a boulder where he could watch the open space below the tank and the land beyond.

Its thirst quenched, the Ovaro wearily hung its head and dozed.

The last gray of twilight faded and darkness spread. Coyotes greeted the night with keening wails. An owl hooted, and once, in the distance, a mountain lion screamed.

All normal sounds of a normal night.

Fargo didn't let it lull his guard. The Apaches were out there, waiting their chance.

He fought to stay awake. Over the past three days he'd barely had three hours of sleep each night and it was taking a toll. Again and again his eyelids grew leaden and his chin dipped to his chest. Again and again he jerked his head up and shook himself.

In the middle of the night a meteor streaked the sky. Some would take that as a bad omen but he wasn't the superstitious sort. He didn't believe black cats were evil, either. Or that breaking a mirror brought seven years bad luck.

His one exception was Lady Luck at the poker table. If he had a mistress, it would be her. What he wouldn't give to be playing cards in a saloon somewhere and sipping fine whiskey. Maybe with a friendly dove at his side. He hadn't been in a saloon in weeks and missed it dearly.

About two hours before sunrise his chin dipped once more, and this time he succumbed to the deep sleep of exhaustion.

A whinny brought Fargo awake with a start. His befuddled brain took note of a pink gleam to the east and the chill morning air, and then he snapped fully awake as he realized he wasn't alone.

The three Apaches had taken advantage of his lapse.

They weren't ten feet away and one had a rifle pointed at his chest.